MARRIA

Trapped in a Far Eastern country on the brink of civil war, Netta could only manage to escape if she married Joss de Courcy—a man she knew only by his reputation, as 'the Fox'. She didn't have much choice in the circumstances—but did he have to treat her as *quite* such a helpless idiot?

Books you will enjoy
by SUE PETERS

CLAWS OF A WILDCAT

'I travel alone. I can't be bothered with encumbrances—however attractive,' Dominic Orr had told Margaret uncompromisingly. But after all, she was a career girl too; her job as a doctor was just as important to her as his as a geologist on an oil rig was to him. So where was the problem?

SHADOW OF AN EAGLE

Why had Marion taken such an immediate and instinctive dislike to Reeve Harland when he turned up to stay in her peaceful valley home? It was almost as if she had some premonition of what he was there for. Yet she didn't know, for quite a long time—and by then it was too late ...

THE STAYING GUEST

Laura had hated having to turn her beloved home into a hotel, but she hadn't had any choice, if she wanted to keep the place at all—and at least there was a certain interest in involving herself with the varied personal problems of her guests. Until Martin Deering arrived, and Laura couldn't think about anyone's problems but her own!

MARRIAGE
IN HASTE

BY

SUE PETERS

MILLS & BOON LIMITED
15–16 BROOK'S MEWS
LONDON W1Y 1LF

First published 1980
Australian copyright 1980
Philippine copyright 1980
This edition 1980

© Sue Peters 1980

ISBN 0 263 73354 8

Set in Linotype Plantin 10 pt. solid

Made and printed in Great Britain by
Richard Clay (The Chaucer Press), Ltd., Bungay, Suffolk

CHAPTER ONE

'I WOULDN'T marry you if you were the last man left on earth!'

Netta faced him defiantly, a tiny figure shaking with outrage, her spirit as fiery as the colour of her copper curls.

'The feeling's mutual,' he snapped back through tight lips. 'Don't imagine I enjoy the prospect of being saddled with you for a wife, for however short a time it may be.'

'Then let's forget the whole crazy idea.'

'There's nothing I'd like better,' he assured her grimly, 'except that I don't relish having the lives of the entire Embassy staff on my conscience for the rest of my days.' Anger rode him like a storm. It blazed through the strange, gold-coloured eyes that earned him the sobriquet 'le Renard' which she was to hear on many lips before she finally reached England, and tightened the lean, brown, pointed face with the wide forehead topped by close-cropped brown curly hair, that would instantly distinguish him in any crowd.

'I'm not responsible for the Embassy staff,' she retorted swiftly.

'Unfortunately I am,' he told her grimly. 'And I'm prepared to go to any lengths to get them away from Lak in safety.'

'Even to the extent of getting married?'

'Even to the extent of marrying you,' he told her with a singular lack of gallantry.

'Why can't you just get them away, and leave me behind?' she cried desperately. She felt blackmailed, trapped. 'I can look after myself.'

'The authorities in Lak don't think so.' His expression said, neither did he. 'They're stretching a point as it is, to allow a plane to land to evacuate the Embassy staff, and their wives and families.' He said 'their wives' with clipped

5

emphasis. 'Their condition was that all the staff must go, or
all must remain here in the Embassy, at the responsibility
of the Ambassador. They refuse to be responsible themselves for individual stray foreigners, they've got quite
enough on their plates as it is, coping with a civil uprising, without bothering with you,' he told her bluntly.
'If you got into difficulties, you'd have to get yourself out
of them, and the authorities aren't prepared to accept blame
for the consequences.'

'But why should they insist I get married, in order to
come on the plane with you?' she demanded angrily. She
would have liked to say, 'get married to you, of all people?'
but she did not quite dare. The flaring light in those
strange gold eyes stopped the words before they were
uttered. 'Why can't I just go on the plane as one of the
Embassy staff, and leave it at that?' she cried instead.

'Because the military have a list of all the bona fide
Embassy staff.' He spoke with the barely controlled patience of someone explaining a point to a witless child.

'You could have told them I was a tourist.'

'And risked you getting shot?' He eyed her incredulously. 'Have you got no conception of the danger you've
placed yourself in, by coming into the country in the first
place?' he demanded. He looked as if he would like to shake
some realisation into her, and Netta caught her breath, but
with a supreme effort of self-control he desisted, and went
on tautly, 'No one would believe you could be simply a
tourist, because no tourist in their right mind would risk
entering a country on the verge of civil war.' His tone
questioned her own sanity, and she flushed angrily, but he
went on before she could speak, 'If you even tried to use
such an explanation, you'd immediately arouse suspicion
that you were a political activator, here to stir up more unrest. And I don't need to point out the penalty for that
kind of behaviour, in Lak,' he finished grimly.

'I came here on business,' she protested angrily.

'They wouldn't accept that, either.' He gave a short,
harsh laugh, and his eyes raked Netta's slender figure, that
remained daintily feminine in spite of her lightweight,

tailored trouser suit. 'Their women don't conduct business. They have the sense to remain at home where they belong, and leave such matters to their menfolk.'

So as well as being an arrogant, overbearing bully, he was a self-confessed male chauvinist. How typical! she thought bitingly.

'I still don't understand why....' She tried to close her mind to the penalties he spoke of. She had heard tales, since she reached the Embassy....

'The only way I could possibly pass off your behaviour to the authorities, and still make it look convincing, was to tell them you were my fiancée, and you'd travelled out here on purpose to marry me. Surprisingly, even a warring army still believes in love.' Did his lips twitch ever so slightly as he said it? She could not be sure.

'You could have told them I was already your wife,' she persisted stubbornly, and his patience snapped.

'After nearly a year in the country, the authorities in Lak know me as well as they know Wendy and Harry Fraser,' he spoke of the Ambassador and his wife, whom Netta had long been friends with, and came to visit while she was in Lak. 'The authorities have got the records of the Embassy....'

'Stole the records, you mean,' she corrected him coldly.

'Have—stole—confiscated—call it what you like, they know I'm a single man.' His voice rose in angry exasperation, and he took a quick step towards her.

Instinctively, Netta stepped backwards, trying to avoid him. In spite of her resolve not to be intimidated, she quailed before his furious glare, but her pace was no match for the length of his arm.

Lean brown fingers like steel bands reached out and circled her wrist. She tried to fling up her arm to free herself, but she was no match for his strength, either. Six feet plus of masculine fury towered over her, provoked out of all patience by her stubborn refusal to obey his order.

And his order was—to marry him! A complete stranger....

'I still don't see why I should be made a sacrifice,' she

made one last frantic bid for her freedom. 'I'm not even on the Embassy staff. I'm only a chance visitor.'

'If you won't see reason,' he gritted, 'you can be the one to tell the Embassy staff just why you think the sacrifice of your maidenly status is worth risking their lives for.'

She had no option but to follow him. He pulled her along behind him with impatient force, through the door of the high-ceilinged Embassy study, and into the big drawing room beyond.

It was crowded with people. Everyone in the Embassy was gathered there, the men accompanied by their wives, and—Netta saw with dismay—a number of young children, ranging from an infant of about six months gurgling on its mother's lap, to a pair of six-year-olds who must be on the verge of being sent back home to school if circumstances had been normal. They all looked up as Jocelyn de Courcey thrust the door open without ceremony and dragged Netta through.

'Any news, Joss?' One of the men spoke up.

'Go on—tell them,' her tormentor grated harshly. 'Tell them—if you can.'

Netta never forgot the hush that followed his words. It was as if everyone in the room held their breath. Then one of the children wailed.

'Daddy, I'm frightened!'

She was about five years old, fair, with curly hair. Two large tears brimmed over, and rolled down her chubby cheeks, and her father reached down to pick her up in his arms, murmuring words of comfort. His eyes met Netta's over the child's head, imploring her....

He was one of the younger aides at the Embassy, the woman with the baby on her lap was his wife. Ordinarily, Netta supposed she would not have got to know them so well, her time would have been taken up with Wendy and Harry, but neither had been able to spare her more than an hour or two since she arrived, and she found herself thrown on the company of the junior staff. Acquaintance-ship ripens quickly under the stress of danger, and she soon got to know them all, and their fears for the safety of their families.

'Daddy, I'm frightened,' the child sobbed.

Her father's gaze held Netta's, anguished, pleading. She could not meet it, could not bear it. It was sheer moral blackmail, but.... She spun to face Joss de Courcey.

'I'll marry you,' she gasped, before she could change her mind.

It was surely the strangest wedding she had ever attended.

'I'll have to go back to my hotel to change into a dress. I can't get married in a trouser suit.'

'There's no time,' Joss objected immediately.

'I shan't defect, if that's what you're afraid of,' she snapped.

'I'm not.' He looked straight at her as he said it, and oddly, she believed him. Believed he trusted her, even if he disliked her. 'There simply isn't time,' he said curtly. 'The plane's due to land just after sundown. We've only got a few hours, and the chief of the military is going to call here to collect me soon to arrange final clearance to release us.' Against her will, she decided he spoke the truth. She felt the same strange sense of trust in him. It was mutual, she decided, the same as their dislike.

'Come and tidy up.' Wendy rescued her, as if she sensed that Netta must have a few moments' respite before she was irretrievably committed. 'You look lovely, just as you are,' her friend comforted her, and Netta rounded on her in amazement.

'You actually approve of this, don't you?' she breathed incredulously. 'Wendy, you're hopeless!' Her knees collapsed as they reached her friend's bedroom, and she sat down on the bed with a rush, torn between a hysterical desire to laugh and cry at the same time. 'You haven't changed a scrap,' she managed at last.

'Well, darling, you must admit it's romantic.' Wendy tried her best to look ashamed, without success.

'Romance!' Netta scoffed. 'You're as bad as when we were teenagers together, at school.'

'Older, maybe,' Wendy conceded with a twinkle, 'but happy with it.' There was no mistaking the light in her eyes, and Netta's lips curved in spite of her own prob-

lems. Wendy's had been a whirlwind romance, with Harry
posted to some out-of-the-way place at the other end of
the earth, and Netta had some misgivings about the marriage lasting, but seven years later they still seemed just as
much in love.

'*You* weren't exactly forced into marriage,' she reminded her friend tartly. 'If only I'd received your cable
in time,' she exclaimed, 'I need never have come to Lak at
all, and the whole wretched affair wouldn't have happened.'

'You must have wondered at my lack of welcome when
you arrived,' Wendy answered ruefully.

'It was a bit of a shock,' Netta admitted. To her astonishment, instead of the effusive greeting she expected, Wendy
received her with frank dismay when she presented herself
at the Embassy.

'Oh, my goodness! Didn't you get my cable, warning
you not to come?'

'No.' Netta looked puzzled for a moment, then en-
lightenment dawned. 'But I haven't been in touch with
London for a couple of weeks or so. Dad's abroad, and
when I had the chance to join a photographic safari it
seemed too good an opportunity to miss. And as it was
only a few days' journey from Lak, I came straight on from
there.' Her friend's lack of response registered, and she
added, 'If you've got a big reception or something on
here, I'll explore by myself for a day or two, until you're
free. We can spend some time catching up on each other's
news afterwards, I needn't go home straight away, I'm not
tied to any particular date of return.'

'You'll return with the Embassy staff the moment Harry
can get clearance for a plane to land,' Wendy cut short her
plans. 'And as for exploring, by yourself or otherwise, forget it,' she advised.

'But why? Is there an outbreak of the plague or something?' Wendy's face, as well as her tone, said she meant
it, and the laugh died in Netta's throat. 'Or are diplomatic
relations strained?' she asked resignedly.

'Neither.' Harry Fraser joined them, and Netta stared

at him, shocked beyond measure at the change in the like-able Scot since she last saw him. He looked exhausted, and desperately worried. 'Lak's asked our help, and we've given all we can, but their government still haven't been able to contain the situation. You've arrived bang in the middle of a civil war,' he informed her baldly.

'So that's why everywhere was so deserted since I crossed the border.' She looked at her two friends, aghast. 'I thought it was probably a fast day, or something, and everyone was either indoors, or in the temples.' The real reason hit her like a blow, and she swallowed hard. 'The proprietor of the hotel was reluctant to give me a room. I wondered why the place was so empty.'

'Everyone who can go has already gone,' the Ambassador told her. 'Where are you booked in at?' he wanted to know.

'In the—that low white building round the corner. I didn't know whether you might have visiting dignitaries at the Embassy, so I got a room to be on the safe side.'

'You should be all right there, until we fly out,' Harry still looked unhappy. 'We'd prefer you to be with us in the Embassy itself, but ...?' He flashed an enquiring glance at his wife.

'There isn't an inch of room to spare here,' Wendy shook her head. 'The French are sharing the place with us until we leave,' she explained. 'Their Embassy up-country has been taken over by the insurgents, and the staff got out just in time, and managed to reach here. Even the bath's being used as a bed,' she wailed despairingly.

'I shall be fine where I am.' Netta hoped she sounded more confident than she felt. 'I'm only a stone's throw away from the Embassy, after all.' She did not know whether she was trying to reassure her friends, or herself.

'Just the same, you must eat your meals with us,' Harry insisted. 'Now you're here, we must keep in constant touch, so that you'll be au fait with any contingency plans we make for evacuating the country in the event the situation deteriorates suddenly.'

'How bad is it?'

'On the boil, but the lid hasn't actually blown off yet,' replied Harry graphically.

'When it does, I hope to goodness we're all on the plane, and on the way home,' Wendy interrupted fervently, and Netta noticed she said 'when' and not 'if'.

'If it were not for le Renard, I think we might not have succeeded in obtaining a plane at all,' one of their French refugee guests put in significantly, and Netta frowned.

'Le Renard?' She looked a question at the Ambassador. 'He sounds sinister, whoever he is,' and she shivered. The Fox. A creature of the night, who came and went with silent tread, along secret paths. 'Surely it isn't necessary for you to have recourse to such a person? A straightforward request from you, to the authorities here....'

'Straightforward requests from an Embassy don't carry much weight in a country torn apart by civil strife,' Harry acknowledged wearily. 'And Jocelyn de Courcey, to give him his correct name, can employ lines of communication which are denied the Embassy.'

'He's not one of your staff, then?' In spite of herself, the peculiar nickname intrigued Netta.

'Officially, he's one of my aides,' Harry said evasively. 'But if you want anything while you're here, ask any of the other aides rather than Joss. He's got other things to do.'

'I think your French guest enjoys a flair for the dramatic.' Netta feigned indifference. Harry obviously did not wish to discuss the mysterious Jocelyn de Courcey any further, and she knew better than to press him. Instead, she shrugged offhandedly. 'Le Renard, indeed!' she scoffed.

'Did you call me, *mademoiselle*?'

He spoke in faultless French, from just behind her. Netta spun round, startled, and found herself looking straight into the strange, golden eyes of the man they called the Fox.

It was like looking straight into the sun. Netta blinked, and had an urge to shut her own lids, as if the light was too bright. Or perhaps to use them as defences, to shut herself away behind them. Hide herself away, might be a better description. The stranger's eyes seemed to bore right through her, laying bare her very thoughts.

'*Non, monsi. . . .*' She stopped herself abruptly. 'I mean —no,' she said firmly, reverting to her own native language with a flash of quite unjustified irritation. Strain was making her edgy, and she felt in no mood to encounter mysterious strangers.

'Ah, Joss, I'm glad you've appeared again.'

Harry was at it now, she thought crossly. First the Frenchman, using such an odd nickname, and now the Ambassador himself saying, 'you've appeared again', instead of, 'you're back', as if the man was some kind of djinn, who could appear and disappear at will. Harry should know better, she thought impatiently, surprised that the normally down-to-earth Scot should succumb to his colleague's flair for drama.

'I want you to meet Netta Vaughan. She'll be coming back on the plane with us,' the Ambassador performed the introductions.

'Miss Vaughan.'

The newcomer acknowledged the introduction with a slight bow, and a look that seemed to pierce right through her. He did not smile, and he did not attempt to shake hands. Netta thrust her own unwanted member back into the pocket of her jacket with angry force, piqued by the omission as he went on, speaking directly to the Ambassador, 'I told the military you had an all-male staff. I must contact them right away, to set things right.'

'Netta isn't on my staff,' Harry said. 'She came to Lak from holiday, to. . . .' He got no further. At the mention of the word holiday, the other man spun round on Netta, and his gold eyes lit with anger.

'You came on holiday—to a country on the verge of civil war?' he snapped incredulously. 'Are you mad?'

His unexpected fury hit her with a solid force, and she recoiled from his verbal attack.

'I—I——' she began, and then her chin came up, and the fiery temper that went with the colour of her hair rose to do battle in her own defence. She drew herself up to her admittedly not very great height, and looked up straight into his face. 'I came here *from* holiday, on a matter of business,' she said haughtily, and wished she was a foot taller, to make her nearer to his height. As it was, her tone failed to crush him as she intended it to, and he interrupted her impatiently.

'Whatever your reason, it can't be of such importance to bring you into Lak at a time like this,' he stormed. 'To risk your life for a triviality....'

'My business is *not* a triviality!' Against life itself, it was, she acknowledged honestly, but she would rather die than admit it to this overbearing stranger.

'Even so, it surely could have waited,' he dismissed her protest as of no consequence. 'To knowingly come across the border into a political cauldron....' Words seemed to fail him. She doubted if they failed him very often, she thought caustically.

'I wasn't aware....'

'The troubles here have been making headlines in every newspaper, television and wireless bulletin in this part of the globe for the past seven days.'

'And for the past fourteen days, I've been out of reach of all three,' she threw back at him triumphantly.

'You must have had to do some pretty convincing talking, to enable you to cross the border post,' he accused her, unimpressed. 'You can't claim ignorance of the situation after that.'

'There was no one manning the border post when I came through.' She had thought it peculiar at the time, but in the absence of anyone there to question, she had little alternative but to drive straight through.

'Surely that struck you as strange?' He gave her no quarter, and his persistence goaded her into an anger to match his own.

'It struck me that the border guards were either drunk, asleep, or had business of their own in the nearby village,' she flung at him rashly.

'They're defecting in droves.' Harry sought to pour oil, but the other man was not to be diverted.

'No matter about the guards,' he dismissed them as

irrelevant. 'Now you're here, you're one more to be got away to safety.' His look, his tone, left her in no doubt he would have preferred there to be one less, and she flushed angrily, then went white.

'You needn't trouble yourself on my account,' she blazed back at him. 'I can look after myself.'

'You may do whatever you please, once you're over the border into peaceful territory,' he informed her icily, 'but while you're in Lak, you're the responsibility of the Embassy, and you'll do exactly as you're told. I'll go and warn the military,' he added to Harry, and spun on his heel.

Before Netta could get her breath back to reply, he was gone. One moment he was there, and the next he had vanished. She stared at where he had been standing, the defiant repudiation of his right to order her to do anything at all, dying on her lips. He was no longer there to defy.

When he returned, it was to tell her she had got to marry him.

CHAPTER TWO

'I've only got his word that he's not married already.' Netta wielded the hairbrush with nervous energy, and Wendy sat up, her eyes round.

'Of course he's not married!' she replied in a scandalised voice. 'Joss is an honourable man. He's one of the Mirshire de Courceys, from Long Minton,' she went on. 'Harry and I have known him for years.'

'He can be one of the de Courceys from Timbuctoo, for all I care,' retorted Netta waspishly.

'Oh, Joss is English enough,' her friend assured her. 'The de Courcey bit might be French—his family go back as far as Agincourt.' She ignored Netta's irreverent mutter, 'I wish they'd stayed there!' and went on, 'He owns Thimbles, now, since the old earl died.'

'Don't say he's got another title as well!' Netta groaned in despair, and Wendy laughed.

'No, the title didn't come down to him. Only Thimbles.'

'Wendy—Netta——' Harry's voice interrupted her discourse, 'Joss is waiting.'

'Let him wait,' Netta muttered, and then the young aide's imploring gaze swam before her mind's eye, and reminded her of the reason for Joss waiting, and she put the brush back on the dressing table.

'Coming!' she called, but her feet dragged as she followed Wendy downstairs, and back into the drawing room. As a concession to the occasion, someone had put two enormous jars of pale golden tua lilies in the room, and their perfume was almost overpowering. 'I think I'll always hate the smell of lilies,' she decided, as her eyes took in the members of the Embassy staff gathered to witness the ceremony. They had been joined by a figure in a strange military uniform, and an elderly man who had the stamp of officialdom indelibly upon him.

'He's the equivalent of a registrar,' Wendy murmured. 'We'd rather have had a priest from the mission, but....'

'The mission?' Netta turned sharply, struck by a sudden idea. 'Couldn't I ...?' she began, and Joss interrupted before she could go any further.

'No,' he refused her adamantly, 'you can't stay at the mission. You're coming back to England with me.' It was only afterwards she remembered he had said, 'with me', and not, 'with us', and wondered why. 'I don't even know your name.' He spoke as if he had thought about it for the first time. 'I take it Netta's short for something, the same as Joss?' There was a hint of humour in his face as he said it.

'It's short for Garnet,' she said stiffly. She could see nothing humorous in the situation.

He inclined his head. 'How appropriate,' he drawled.

Was he being sarcastic? She eyed him suspiciously.

'Harry's been telling me your background,' he said smoothly. So he had pumped Harry about her, just the same as she had pumped Wendy about him! They were even on that score, at least, she thought with a touch of malice. He would know, now, that her father was John Vaughan, the renowned jeweller and goldsmith. If he thought any further along the same lines, he might also guess what her business was in Lak, she realised uneasily. So long as he did not guess the details. As if in a dream she stood beside him in front of the elderly official, and heard his firm voice declare,

'I, Jocelyn, take thee, Garnet ... for better, for worse....'

'For better, for worse—but not for long,' Netta added a silent rider of her own. The moment they were back in England, and safe....

'To love and to cherish....' He could forget that, too, she thought fiercely. She would be his wife in name only until they reached safety. Because he was marrying her, it did not automatically give him any rights or privileges.

He turned and slid a slender gold ring from off his own little finger, and with a firm clasp raised her left hand and slipped it on. Amazingly, it fitted. His own fingers were slender, and the exchange made a perfect match. The gold band still felt warm from his own hand. Netta looked down at the intricately chased surface, and her training under her father told her the ring was very old. In all probability it was a family heirloom. She would return it to Joss, later. . . .

Without warning, the ring swam in front of her vision, and her heart wept within her. No marriage should take place like this, it protested. Marriage should not be a thing of expediency, after a moment's acquaintance. It was something precious, to be born from love, and tended by time. Marriage was for ever. . . .

She had always planned to marry, if she did so at all, in the little church they attended close to their London home, with herself in white, and her father to give her away. Not a cold, unemotional, civil ceremony like this. She blinked hard and began to tremble, and then felt her hand clasped between two firm brown ones, which closed about it, warming her fingers. It was as if Joss sensed what she might be feeling, and gave her what reassurance he could. She clutched his fingers convulsively, in a surge of unexpected gratitude, and heard the official say, 'I now pronounce you man and wife.' And realised, with a dreadful sense of finality, what it was she had done.

'Try and look as if you're pleased, the military are watching.'

He turned her towards him and growled a warning under cover of claiming a bridegroom's privilege—his first kiss. She supposed it should not have surprised her under the circumstances, he had to make the ceremony look as genuine as possible, but somehow it did. He bent his head above her, and she raised her face dutifully, if reluctantly, to meet the firm, hard pressure of his lips. An impersonal pressure, placed there to satisfy tradition, and the watching soldiery.

But tradition did not demand that his lips should linger on her own, exploring their untried sweetness. And then, without warning, change, and become fired with an urgent, demanding passion that took her completely by surprise. It ran like lightning through her veins, tingling her every nerve end into a startled awareness of the man who held her in his arms. Her husband.... For a second or two she lay quiescent in his embrace, and then the slumbering womanhood that until this moment had lain dormant during all her twenty-six years burst forth into lovely blossom, warmed into life by the power of his kiss. She was powerless to resist. Helplessly, she felt herself returning kiss for kiss, drawn into a response she did not know it was in her power to give until, in one brief, heart-stopping moment, Joss de Courcey taught her how.

When at last he raised his head, she did not need to dissemble to dupe the military. Her face glowed, and her eyes shone, polished to brilliance by the solemn vows she had just taken, and the crazy, wonderful, impossible conviction that she did not regret any one of them.

A full minute passed before Joss's warning came back to her. A full minute in which he looked deep into her eyes, reading her feelings as plainly as if he might read a book, though she was unable to even try to interpret his own, because of the daze of conflicting emotions which she had never experienced before, and did not know how to handle now.

'The military are watching....' As if to underline his warning, the figure in uniform approached them.

'Congratulations, Mrs de Courcey.'

She heard her married name spoken for the first time. The soldier did not smile as he said it. His eyes regarded her with a hard, unfriendly, official stare, and without warning Netta went cold from head to foot. Not from fear of the soldier, or the thought of the ceremony just behind her, and the fact that now she was Joss's wife, but at the realisation of what Joss himself had done to her.

'Try and look as if you're pleased,' he told her. And to add realism to the ceremony, he kissed her. Not because he wanted to, but to impress the soldiers. The urgent passion that awakened her response was nothing but playacting, on his part. It was done with consummate skill, and bitter recrimination flooded her at his betrayal. He need not have gone so far, even to convince the military. His over-enthusiasm had not only convinced the soldiers— momentarily, it had succeeded in convincing her, Netta, as well. And once a flower has opened to the sun, it can never again retreat into an unawakened bud. . . .

The realisation of what he had done extinguished the shine from her eyes and the glow from her face. It drained the newly awakened vitality from her heart, and left it as hollow as an empty cowrie shell, to be occupied by an agony of pain such as she had never known before. In a daze she felt Joss put his arm round her waist—the act of any normal bridegroom—and desperately she forced herself not to flinch away. The soldier was still watching. She leaned against her new husband, involuntarily adding realism to her own performance, but it was because her legs felt suddenly weak, not because she wanted to. She felt she would rather lean against any other person in the room, even the soldier, than rely on Joss for support.

'He shouldn't have done this to me.'

Out of the depths of pain and misery, a burning anger rose inside her against the man who had just made her his wife. She longed to tear off his ring and throw it back at him, deny her newly acquired status. Her right hand moved to do her bidding, and then her eyes caught the eyes of the soldier, still watching her, noting her every reaction, and drawing conclusions from it, and instead her shaking fingers turned the ring round and round on her finger, twisting it in an excess of nervous energy, but leaving it in place. She lowered her eyes, unable to stand the soldier's stare any longer, and found they looked down on her ring instead, so she raised them again, hating the thin gold circle, and forced herself to meet the stare without flinching.

'Wait for me here. I'll come back for you when the plane's ready to leave.'

She heard Joss speak to her, and then he kissed her again, lightly this time, playing the loving husband, she thought bitterly. She felt his lips brush her forehead, but the contact hardly registered through the turmoil of conflicting emotions that rocked the very fibre of her being.

'Go and finish packing.' Harry spoke to Wendy, reverting to mundane matters. The ceremony was over, the knot tied—Netta felt as if it choked her—but everyday things must be attended to. Her heart had just died within her, but ... 'Go and finish packing....' A hysterical laugh caught at her throat, and died as the soldier paused on his way to the door with Joss.

'There will only be space in the plane for light hand luggage,' he warned the room in general. 'No one must take any more than is absolutely necessary for overnight,' he instructed sternly, and gave Harry a significant look as he added, 'All baggage will be searched, to make sure you comply.'

'That means I can't take any office records with me.' Harry frowned at the closing door, and turned swiftly to his aide as soon as the soldier disappeared. 'Come, we've no time to lose. All our files must be destroyed before we leave.'

'I'll get what we need, right away.' Wendy moved too, then turned back impulsively to Netta. 'This is criminal, darling. Just as you're married!' she wailed.

'It was hardly a love match,' Netta reminded her tartly. She stirred herself reluctantly into action, forcing herself to appear as normal as possible. She heard her lips form the lie, and a small, detached part of her mind wondered how she could. Until now, she had never believed in love at first sight. That was something which belonged to magazine romances. Now, she knew it could happen—to her, if not to Joss. It was Joss's fault, for rousing her. There was no need for him to do this to her, even to convince the soldiers. In one moment of blinding revelation she discovered what it was to love. And what it was to hate....

'I'll go and get some things from the hotel,' she heard herself respond to Wendy. She would want some overnight things the same as the others. And she also wanted the package she had collected when she first came to Lak, the package which was the sole reason for her coming at all. But Wendy was already on her way upstairs in Harry's wake, and Netta did not know whether she had heard her or not.

'Your baggage will be searched....'

The soldier's barb had been directed at Harry, but it found a dual target, she thought grimly. At all costs she was determined not to be parted from the contents of her package. But how could she conceal them, to escape a baggage search? It had all seemed so simple, when she played hostess to her father's client in the tall Georgian house in the quiet London square, less than a month ago.

'I'll collect the pieces of jewellery you want re-set, Ranjit.' Over the years her father's client had become his friend, and they had long been on first name terms. 'You say you aren't likely to be in England again until next spring, and if I travel out for them it'll give me time to do the work for you, and have them ready for when you come again. How much work is there involved?' She glanced across the tea table at her father.

'The same as before,' the white-haired goldsmith answered her. 'We have to substitute synthetic stones for the real gems, and use the original settings if we can. I'll have to look at the settings to see what condition they're in.' He turned to his client. 'You tell me some of the pieces have been in your family for generations, and are much worn. The enamelled pieces should be all right, but the gold settings are softer, and may have become thin with long use.'

'We can copy them for you,' Netta put in, with the un-troubled confidence that only skill can bestow.

'If we have to,' her father nodded. 'Ranjit's brought some excellent photographs, and full dimensions of the pieces. If necessary we could make perfect copies, just from those.' He looked an enquiry at his client.

'I should still want the jewellery to come to London,' Ranjit objected. 'It has to be deposited in my bank here.'

'In that case,' Netta smiled, 'expect me in Lak shortly after you get back home from your business trip here. I'll collect the pieces and bring them back to London, and we can do all the rest for you here. I still think it's a pity, though,' she reflected.

It was a common enough commission nowadays, but she could not help regretting the necessity to hide the beauty of the real gems within the unappreciative walls of a bank vault. Even after the substitute synthetic gemstones were in place, the pieces of jewellery would still be extremely valuable. Modern laboratory-made gem crystals were costly imitations of nature's products, and the work involved in cutting and polishing was just as exacting as on the real stones. Nevertheless. . . . She sighed.

'It's a good deal safer to wear the synthetics,' her father reminded her, but in his eyes, too, there was a trace of lingering regret. Although he was world-renowned, and numbered royalty among his clients, he still retained a love for the basic materials of his trade that neither affluence nor familiarity could dispel.

'I don't feel too happy about you collecting those pieces from Ranjit, Netta,' to her surprise her father frowned concernedly after their client left that evening. 'There are rumours of unrest in Lak.'

'There's unrest everywhere, even in our own country.' Netta dismissed his fears lightly. 'There's always somebody disagreeing with somebody else over something,' she stated not too clearly. She often acted as her father's courier on such errands, and felt puzzled at his objection now. 'If it makes you any happier, I intend to contact Wendy and Harry Fraser at the Embassy when I get there —it's years since I saw them both, not since they were sent out to Lak from Paris.'

'In that case. . . .' Her father's face cleared. 'You won't have a great deal to carry in the way of weight,' he went on more happily. 'From what Ranjit told me, most of the pieces consist of rings and pendants, with a few bracelets and hair ornaments. All of it's his wife's jewellery, and all fairly small.'

Even so, it was big enough to become a problem, now she was faced with a baggage search. She began to wish for the first time that she had not overridden Ranjit's objections when she called to see him to collect it soon after her arrival.

'I daren't give it to you,' he told her worriedly. 'With all this unrest in the country, it might put you at risk.' Endearingly, he was more concerned about the risk to her than to his possessions.

'There'll be no risk at all to me,' Netta persuaded. 'I'm travelling out with the Embassy staff. What better escort could your gems possibly have than a plane load of diplomats?' she pressed. 'And Harry Fraser says there's been widespread looting in the north. If the insurgents laid hands on your wife's jewellery....' She paused significantly.

'They would use it to fund their evil cause,' Ranjit finished for her, and his face grew stern. 'I'd do much to prevent that from happening.'

The alternative left him with no real choice. Which was how Netta came to have her present problem of smuggling the jewellery out of the country, a totally unnecessary subterfuge if times had been normal. She thought about confiding her problem to Harry, and enlisting his help, then decided against it.

'He's got enough worries of his own, without adding mine to them.'

The thought of Joss occurred to her, and she shook her head fiercely.

'Never!' she declared out loud. 'He'd simply make me take them back to Ranjit.' The very possibility hardened her resolve to find some way—any way—to keep the jewellery with her, and to convey it to safety in England as she had promised. She had never yet let down one of her father's clients, and she did not intend to do so now, Joss or no Joss, she determined.

She remembered as she sped through the eerily deserted streets that Joss had told her to remain at the Embassy until he came back for her. Well, Joss would have to lump it if he did not like her disobedience, she decided. She needed some overnight things, the same as the rest of the

Embassy staff, and the streets were empty, so there could be no immediate danger. The first person she saw, in fact, was the hotel proprietor, who left his task of boarding up his ground floor windows with obvious reluctance, to retrieve her package for her from his office safe.

'I'm leaving as soon as I've packed,' Netta told him briefly, and the relief on his face added to her disquiet. She knew, now, what it felt like to be a foreigner in a country at war. Neither side loved foreigners. They were a nuisance, in the way, and to be despatched out of that way with all possible speed. To his credit, the man tried to be helpful, but he had problems of his own, like the imminent danger of smashed windows, looters, and rapidly deserting staff. He could not hide his relief at the news of her departure.

'I'll be half an hour,' Netta told him, and gained her room with a sigh of relief. She needed solitude in which to collect herself after the events of the last few hours. The sounds of a hammer and nails being wielded on boards to protect the downstairs windows of the building told her that her need could not be indulged. Rapidly she slit open the package that Ranjit had given to her and spread the contents on the bed. She fingered through the glittering heap with growing dismay.

'I can't possibly conceal all this lot!'

The soldier promised a baggage search, but she could not discount the possibility of a personal search as well. The jacket of her trouser suit had short sleeves and a shirt neckline, and she was wearing no jewellery except her watch during the marriage ceremony, something that could not have escaped the notice of the watching soldier. The big patch pockets of her jacket were too obvious to even be considered; they were the first places any searcher would look at. And to attempt to board the plane actually festooned with Ranjit's wife's jewellery would be simply asking for trouble. The settings were traditional, and worn by their owner to adorn her sari they would go unremarked except for their outstanding beauty. But worn by Netta, to accompany a safari suit? No, the idea was unthinkable. She knitted her brows in perplexity.

Finally she shrugged, then reached for her travelling manicure set, and blessed the makers for its stout construction. There was no help for it. It was sheer vandalism, but.... She set doggedly to work with one of the tools. Several times the sharp-pointed instrument slipped, but she gritted her teeth and ignored the welling scratches across her hands, and continued ruthlessly to uproot the gemstones from their lovely settings.

'Dad wanted to know what condition the settings were in,' she muttered. Their conversation returned to reproach her for wreaking such destruction. 'Now I'll be able to report that they're damaged beyond repair.' The gold settings did not present so much difficulty, they were softer, but the enamelled pieces were hard, and the gemstones consequently much more difficult to extricate, so that her struggles resulted in the settings suffering more from her hurried ministrations. At her work bench in London, with proper tools, and time at her disposal, they would not even have shown a scratch.

She winced as she looked at the discarded pile rapidly growing on the bed on the one side of her. 'Thank goodness Ranjit had the forethought to bring with him photographs and dimensions of the pieces, when he came to London,' she breathed thankfully. 'At least we'll be able to reproduce them accurately.'

'It's wicked, I know, but I can't help it,' she murmured at last, in apology to the long-dead jeweller whose hands had framed the beauty she now so wantonly wrecked.

'Thank goodness that's over!' She swept up the settings into a small pile at the back of a drawer, and covered them with clothes. There were not many to cover them with, she travelled light, but rumpled up they were sufficient to conceal the settings. She doubted if looters would bother with female fripperies, even if they managed to enter the barricaded building, and there was simply nowhere else she could conceal them. She had never realised before how bare a hotel room could be; even the wardrobe had no frontage on the top, it was completely flat, and would not conceal a fly.

'What on earth shall I do with these?'

She considered the small pile of gemstones that was left—rubies, emeralds, diamonds, of she dared not think what value. They winked back at her from the bed cover with solemn mockery, taunting her with their beauty—their priceless worth—and her own despairing inability to think of a single hiding place about her person, which seemed as lacking as the hotel room of reasonable possibilities that would not be immediately obvious to a suspicious soldier.

Her fingers fidgeted nervously with the waistband of her slacks. They felt damp with her recent efforts, and she rubbed them on the cloth to dry them. The dampness stuck to the material, moving it with her fingers, making the double cloth of the band rub up and down against itself, and she paused, struck by a sudden idea.

'The waistband of my slacks!' she breathed. 'Why didn't I think of that right away?' Indecision had already wasted precious minutes. The band was wide, and shaped, and in effect a continuous tube running right round her waist, the ends closed by the zip, and ideal for the purpose she had in mind.

She reached for her nail scissors and began snipping the end stitching of the belt. If she could slide the gemstones into the tube, they were small enough not to make too much of a bulge in the cloth, and might pass a perfunctory search. She tried the first one, and realised she would not get them in easily with her slacks still on. Quickly she wriggled out of them, and began pushing the gems one by one into the waistband with feverish haste, sliding them along, so that they were more or less evenly spaced, and did not bunch up together. She had told the hotelier she would be half an hour. She must have already been that, and more. If she did not hurry, he might come upstairs, demanding to know when she would be gone. As if to confirm her fears, a loud knocking on her bedroom door made her jump, and a voice demanded to know when she would be ready to go.

'Don't come in, I'm not dressed!' she called out, and after a slight pause she heard his feet shuffle away along the corridor, his voice muttering impatiently. It would not do to try his tolerance too far. The thought added impetus to her efforts. With fingers that shook, so that she had to make three attempts to thread the needle, she stitched the end of the waistband together again, careful to make a good job of it so that the stitches did not show, even if it took a good extra two minutes to accomplish.

'These are the most valuable slacks I've ever worn,' she grinned suddenly as she put them on again, and paused in the act of tucking her shirt inside the band. If it was left outside, it would be an even better concealment, and it was fashionable, so it would not cause comment. She pulled the silk out again, then without hesitation stripped the shirt straight back over her head. The material was creased. It had obviously been tucked into the band, and the soldiers, suspicious already, might guess. Hurriedly she took another top from the drawer and slid it over her head. It was loose and clean, and uncreased, and long enough to come down to her hips, which was an added bonus, she saw with satisfaction.

'There's only my holiday film now.' She was reluctant to leave that behind. During the safari she had taken clips of many exotic flowers she had never seen before. They would give her inspiration for unusual brooch designs, a speciality which was making her almost as well known as her father. 'It's no good taking the camera, they're almost certain to confiscate that.' And she dared not take any clothes, either, or there would be nothing with which to conceal the jewel settings. She cast a reluctant look at her expensive photographic equipment, and turned her back resolutely on her undies as an imperative knocking sounded on her door. Hurriedly she thrust the clip of film underneath the loose change in her purse, picked up her shoulder bag, and opened the door to the proprietor's worried entreaties.

'You must go now, missie. Go quickly,' he urged. He looked very frightened, as if he wished he could take his own advice. 'Not that way,' he checked her as she made for the main stairway. 'Through the back. . . .' He chivvied her along a corridor and through what looked like kitchen quarters. She could not be sure what they were, in the dim light which was all the newly boarded windows allowed through. She had no clear idea in which direction she was heading, and then her guide unlocked a small door and shooed her through.

'Go quickly,' he urged again. 'They come....' And he slammed the door behind her. Netta heard the key turn in the lock, with a finality that told her there would be no going back.

She turned and looked about her apprehensively. She was in a narrow alley, presumably at the rear of the hotel that must, she judged, run parallel with the main street by which she had arrived. She would have to hurry. A quick glance at her watch told her it was not long to sundown, and she still had to get back to the Embassy. She could see the tip of its roof from where she stood, but it would take her a good ten minutes to get there along the streets, by which time she stood the risk of being caught by the curfew which Harry told her had been imposed during the emergency, and the even greater risk of keeping the others waiting for the plane.

CHAPTER THREE

WHICH way should she go?

Netta looked from side to side along the alleyway, un-decided. One way seemed as good as the other. The alley twisted, so that she could not see either end. Without con-scious choice, she turned right. If she was careful to skirt the sides of the hotel she should reach the main road even-tually.

'If I'm wrong, I can always turn back,' she told herself.

There was not really time. She looked about her anxi-ously, hoping to find a short cut, but the properties that backed on to the alley all seemed to be enclosed by high walls, so that she had to keep to the pedestrian way, whether she wanted to or not. Nervously, she skirted the umpteenth deep, shadowed doorway, keeping to the middle of the alley, heart thumpingly conscious of the precious cargo she carried about her waist.

Her breath came in short pants, partly from haste, but mostly from tension, and perhaps a little, though she re-fused to admit it even to herself, perhaps a little from fear of what Joss might say if he returned to the Embassy and found her missing, when he had expressly instructed her to wait for him there.

She neared the end of the alley and sounds began to penetrate the high walls. She paused. Vehicle brakes squealed from somewhere ahead, and a man's voice rose in an unknown tongue.

'Even out here, they've got their share of careless drivers,' she grinned, and went on again, feeling more re-laxed. Harry said most of the townspeople had fled, but there must be some still left. They were probably trying to do the same as she was herself, reach home before the curfew. Perhaps one of them might know of a short cut back to the Embassy. In another ten minutes it would be dark, with the sudden, total darkness of the tropical night, and she did not relish the thought of being out alone after that.

She reached the end of the alley, which led, as she suspected, back on to the main street, though slightly farther along, at the other side of a small square, which in peaceful times must make a pleasant promenade for the residents. The cause of the noise she had heard became immediately apparent. A number of lorries of doubtful make and vintage were drawn up in the square, higgledy-piggledy, with no attempt at orderly parking, and men were disembarking by the simple expedient of vaulting over the sides on to the ground. They must be estate workers, she judged, there were plantations on the edge of the town, and these must be the pickers returning after their day's labours.

'I wouldn't like to work for him!' One man, presumably their leader, harangued the others. Netta could not understand what he said, but he seemed to be urging speed, although the men in the lorries were wasting no time in vacating their transport. 'Bully!' she muttered, as he shouted again, and then he swung his arm, and her horrified eyes caught sight of what looked like a length of chain dangling from his hand. 'Surely he doesn't ...?' She stared at the group of workers crowding near him, but they did not appear to be in any way intimidated. Rather, his gestures seemed to arouse them to the same pitch of hysteria that he himself displayed. Several began to shout and gesticulate as well, and the group broke up and began to move across the square.

'They've all got weapons!'

The appalling truth broke upon her like a douche of cold water. They were not plantation pickers; they were a mob of insurgents. The maître d' hotel had said, when he thrust her through his door into the alley, 'They come. . . .'

'He's wrong,' she thought, panic-stricken, 'they've already arrived!'

Without hesitation, she turned and ran. Her heart beat with a terror that made its previous nervous palpitations seem like a gentle murmur, and she clutched at her side, doubled up by an unbearable stitch. The pain of it slowed her down, but the shouts of the men in the square drove her on until she rounded the bend of the alley.

'They've come in at both ends!' Her breath sobbed in her throat, and she stumbled to a terrified halt, leaning against the wall for support, and stared aghast at the shouting rabble that crowded into the entrance to the alley- way in front of her. Unknown to her, the narrow pedestrian passageway must describe a horseshoe round the back of the hotel, and both ends led on to the main street. And the rebels had entered it at either end.

She had often wondered what the word 'insurrection' really meant. She had glanced at it casually on the small print of insurance forms in clauses indemnifying the in- surers from, '... the consequences of ... rebellion, re- volution, insurrection, or military or usurped power....' Now she knew at first hand what those words implied. The mob were approaching her from both sides, incited to near-hysteria by the yells of their leader, and they were armed to the teeth, and intent on trouble. And she car- ried Ranjit's jewels around her waist. She was trapped.

'The door back into the hotel.' The mob had not seen her yet. Her sand-coloured trouser suit nearly matched the colour of the walls, and it made an excellent camouflage so long as she did not make any exaggerated movement to draw attention to herself.

She flattened herself against the wall and inched care- fully back along the way she had come, round the bend, and out of sight, for the moment anyway, of the men coming towards her. She blessed the fact that the alley was so narrow, it slowed their pace as they crowded into the entrance. If she could reach the door into the back of the hotel.... Surely the proprietor would not refuse to let her in? He *must* let her in! The doorway loomed beside her, and she turned into the archway which sheltered it, and raised her fist to beat a tattoo on the wood.

'It's the wrong colour!'

She stared at the paintwork with numb disbelief. The

hotel door had been bright blue, and freshly painted. This one had peeling paint, of a colour long since faded into anonymity by age and neglect.

'It must be the next door,' she muttered.

It seemed like a hundred miles to the next door, although it could only have been a few yards in reality. The cries of the mob behind her grew louder, and she caught her breath, panic beginning to numb her mind, destroy her power to think. The threatening roar from the opposite end of the alley was getting louder, too. It only needed one of the rebels from either side of her to round the bend, and they could not fail to see her.

She sprang across to the other side of the alley, to hug the bend of the wall more closely. At least she would delay discovery as long as she could. It would be easy enough to cross back when she was opposite to the next doorway, she could see it a few yards along. There was a door on her side, as well, but she ignored it. The dark shadowed aperture of the archway held fewer terrors for her now than the approaching pincer movement of the insurgents. She reached the edge of the door arch on her side, and....

'Don't scream!'

An arm reached out of the darkness of the archway. It wrapped tentacle-like about her waist, and dragged her into the shadows. A hand clamped over her mouth, stifling the scream that rose to her lips regardless of his warning, which his hold rendered unnecessary anyhow. His hand clamped over her nose, too, so that she could not breathe. She started to struggle.

'Keep still,' a deep voice growled impatiently, 'unless you'd rather be caught by that mob out there.'

Shock immobilised her, not the order. The voice spoke in cultured English. And it belonged—she was sure it belonged to——

'Joss!' she whispered.

'Be quiet!' he ordered her tersely, in her ear, and lifted her bodily through the doorway, silently sliding the bolts to behind them the moment it was closed.

'But how—why ...?'

For answer, he kissed her. His lips closed on hers, parting them with a fierce urgent pressure, and she lost the desire to ask questions. The passionate woman inside her, whom Joss first aroused—was it only a few short hours ago?—and whom Netta herself had not yet even begun to know, came to life again at the touch of his lips. She tried to steel herself against him, but it was useless. Her senses throbbed with his nearness, and without conscious thought her arms rose to clasp his head, feeling the brown curls surprisingly soft under her stroking fingers.

From the other side of the wall, the clamour of the mob rose to deafening proportions as the two groups met in the narrow passageway, but it was as nothing to the clamour of her heart.

It sang inside her breast with a wild, vibrant song of uninhibited joy, that was at the same time as tender as a crooning lullaby. It hushed her fears and her protests and her questions, and she melted into his arms, turning her face upwards to meet his kisses with an eagerness that matched the fierce passion of his lips, uncaring that the shouts rose to a crescendo on the other side of the wall, and then grew dim and finally died away as the mob, finding nothing but an empty alley, surged off in search of more likely prey.

'Joss. . . .' Her voice was a soft whisper when at last he let her go.

'That's the only way I know to keep a woman quiet,' he said. And he laughed.

The merciful darkness hid her face. It sheltered the stunned shock that blanched her cheeks and lips, and left her eyes bleak with the bleakness of someone who in a few short hours has been awakened for the first time to the full, wondrous glory of love—and learned as well to feel the destroying corrosion of hate. And come by the same road to the bitter knowledge that, far from being two separate emotions, the two could well be one.

'I hate you!'

She felt him pause, and look down at her in the darkness.

'It didn't feel like that a few minutes ago.' His voice mocked her, a disembodied taunt from somewhere over her head. It stung her into impulsive action, and she pushed against him with all her strength, freeing herself from his arms. Loathing his touch.

'Go away,' she cried. 'Leave me alone!'

'Keep your voice down!' His own voice hissed like a whip through the darkness, lashing her into silence. 'D'you want to bring that mob howling at our heels?' he growled angrily. His hands left her waist and gripped her by her wrists, cruelly tight.

'Loose me. Let me go!' She whispered the words, the threat of tears as much as the threat of the mob choking back her voice.

'I'll do nothing of the kind.' His voice tightened, and so did his grip. 'You're coming with me.'

'You can't make me.'

He proceeded to demonstrate that he could. He loosened her one wrist, but kept tight hold of the other, and pulled her with him through what appeared to be a courtyard, then paused at another door to whisper back, 'Whether you love me or loathe me is quite irrelevant. Every moment the plane remains on the airstrip waiting for us increases the danger of its being taken by the rebels. I won't have the other passengers put at risk because of you,' he told her sternly, then broke off, and against the paler wall she could faintly see his head raised in a listening attitude. She held her breath and listened, too. 'In case you don't know, that's gunfire,' he enlightened her grimly as the distant popping sounds continued. 'And it's coming this way. It's time we left.'

She might as well try to resist a tornado, she thought despairingly, then another burst of gunfire split the night, and voices began to shout. Someone screamed.

All thoughts of resisting Joss vanished. She sped alongside him, conscious that his grip on her wrist slackened, as if he sensed she would comply now, and follow him, simply using his hold to guide her. He led her with silent speed across a bewildering number of walled courtyards;

through endless doors and along alleyways until she lost all sense of direction. Joss seemed to know exactly where he was, and the way he wanted to go, and in spite of the almost total darkness he did not hesitate once. He found his way with an uncanny exactitude, unhampered by the lack of light, like a wild creature that dons the cloak of the dark for protection.

'Le Renard.' He lived up to his odd nickname.

'What is it?' He paused, and she panted to a stop beside him.

'Nothing—never mind.' She did not realise she had spoken out loud.

'Then keep up with me. And keep quiet.'

More doors. More courtyards. More alleyways, until——

'Down!'

Even as he flung her to the ground, she felt the vibration through the earth, seconds before she heard the bang. Joss's mercurial reaction saved them. He threw her under the shelter of the nearest wall, and himself on top of her, and the blast of the explosion whistled harmlessly past above their heads. It must have met resistance further along the alley, because sounds of crashing masonry and splintering glass echoed back to them, a grim reminder of what their own fate could have been if Joss had not....

'Are you hurt?' He pulled her to her feet without ceremony.

'No.' She shook her head, too shaken to talk.

'Then come.' He waited for no more, but he loosed her hand.

'Joss....' She held it out to him, appealingly, suddenly desperate for the reassurance of his touch, but he ignored it, and grasped her round the waist, supporting her, but also, she realised, forcing her to keep up with his now much greater pace. The stitch returned to her side, but a spreading glow from the fire against the sky was sufficient to anaesthetise the pain. She ran beside him until, just as she began to fear she could not go on any longer, a breeze stroked her face, and Joss slackened his pace to a walk. She lifted her face to the welcome breath. True, it carried the acrid taint of burning, but it was better than the stifling, airless heat of the alleys. Those lay behind them, she could see the outline of the high walls making strange, geometric patterns against the glow in the sky. A flat expanse of open land lay before them.

'The airstrip.' Joss located their whereabouts for her.

'Thank goodness!' she breathed. Soon they would be on their way to safety.

'Keep low, and stay by me.' Joss ducked and turned into the rough scrub bordering the edge of the airstrip, using it as a cover to prevent their figures from showing up against the glow from the fires in the town, which seemed to Netta to grow alarmingly brighter with every minute.

'There's no need to push me into the ground!' she snapped. He had chosen a route that would enable them to run side by side, and his arm pressed relentlessly against her back, forcing her to crouch double as she ran.

'Wait!'

He dropped down on one knee, obliging her to do the same, and the thorny scrub pierced the thin stuff through the knees of her slacks.

'Ouch!'

'Silence!' he hissed. 'Look. . . .'

She heard the engines burst into life even as he turned her, in time to see the aircraft itself, a pale shape in the darkness ahead of them, begin to move across the open airstrip.

'That's our plane.' The one that was waiting for them. The one that should take them to safety.

'The pilot probably got tired of waiting,' Joss retorted sharply. 'Under the circumstances, I can't say I blame him.' His tone blamed Netta. 'Get ready to run,' he warned her before she could speak, 'he'll probably taxi out this way, and if we can manage to attract his attention. . . .'

'You mean, we flag him down, like a bus?' A sharp giggle rose in her throat at the incongruity of his suggestion, and she stifled it hastily. If the pilot did not see them, if he left them behind, there would be nothing to giggle about. She tensed herself to rise, and then everything seemed to happen at once.

'Down!'

Joss's hand on her back thrust her flat with a force that knocked the breath from her lungs. A loud barrage of shots from somewhere on the other side of the plane drowned her angry protest. They were quickly followed by a flash, and an explosion, and Joss half rose to his knees.

'Take off, you fool! Take off,' he begged of the pilot.

Engines roared to a crescendo as if in answer to his bidding. Men shouted. A fusillade of shots rang out, and the pale shape of the aircraft thundered towards them with a deafening roar. Netta ducked, convinced it could not rise in time, and then the wheels left the ground in an almost vertical take-off that brought a desperate mutter from Joss.

'He's got to make it! He's got to. . . .'

The engines screamed with the strain, but somehow, miraculously, they held, and gradually the pale cylinder gained height, and rose out of gunshot range above their heads, into the safety of the sky.

'Phew!' Joss subsided into the scrub beside her. 'That was a close call.'

'They've left us behind.' Her voice was a thin thread of fear.

'It's your own fault,' he rounded on her harshly. 'I told you to remain at the Embassy until I came back for you.'

'I'd have been back there before dark if it hadn't been for the mob in town,' she retorted defiantly, refusing to accept his blame.

'If you'd remained at the Embassy, you'd have been there when the news came that the insurgents had already reached the town.'

'Harry said they were forty miles away.'

'Harry didn't know then that they'd commandeered a fleet of trucks which made short work of your forty miles,' he enlightened her grimly. 'The moment the news came through, the Embassy was evacuated. Fortunately, Wendy remembered you saying something about going to collect some clothes from the hotel, otherwise I wouldn't have known where you'd gone. As it was, I wasted a good deal of timing in looking for you. From now on,' he ordered brusquely, 'you'll remain with me, and do exactly what I tell you to.'

'There's no earthly reason why I should.' Even in her present plight she resented his overbearing attitude, and her tone said so plainly.

'In case you've forgotten,' he reminded her in a hard voice, 'a few hours ago you promised to love, honour, and obey me. And until we're safely away from Lak, I intend to see you do just that,' he stated uncompromisingly.

Love, honour—and obey. He meant the latter, of course. The love and honour part did not count; he had not married her for love.

Slow tears invaded her defences. They scalded her cheeks in the darkness, and she turned her head away so that Joss should not see and dropped it wearily on to her arms, careless of the thorny shrubs that surrounded them. The thorns could not inflict any greater pain than the desolation which tore at her heart.

The receding sound of the aircraft droned away into the distance, heading towards the border. It mocked her plight, and mocked the bitter realisation that, now the plane had left without them, she need not have married Joss in the first place.

CHAPTER FOUR

'I FEEL as if I've begun to take root here!'

Netta groaned and eased herself stiffly on to her knees, following Joss's lead. She felt cramped, and cold, and sore all over, particularly around her waist, and she blamed Joss bitterly for being the cause of her discomfort.

'We've only been here for an hour or two.' To her chagrin he remained completely unmoved by her plight.

'He's incapable of feeling,' she told herself angrily, incensed by the fact that Joss himself showed no signs of suffering from any discomfort. 'It doesn't feel like that to me,' she said aloud. They seemed to have lain flat in the scrub for days instead of just hours. She shivered, and eased her fingers under her slacks belt. The gemstones she had so ruthlessly extracted from their settings were small and fairly flat to look at, but they felt just the reverse to lie on, she thought ruefully.

'What's the matter with your waist?'

'Nothing.' She had not realised he might notice her movement. She would have to be careful, he must not guess. 'I'm tightening my belt,' she answered him tartly. She felt both cold and very hungry.

'It's your own fault you've gone without food,' he offered her scant sympathy. 'If you'd waited at the Embassy as I told you to, you'd probably be sitting down to a good meal on the plane by now.'

'You'll blame me for the uprising next,' she accused him hotly, stung by his tone.

'I don't blame you for that,' he conceded, and amazingly she detected a note of amusement in his voice, 'though it was probably a woman who started it.'

'You....'

'There's no point in starting another war,' he checked her furious retort. 'You can't win, and it's bad policy to go

40

into battle on an empty stomach,' he taunted. He rose to his feet, and his head turned, his eyes searching the surrounding darkness. 'There's no sign of the mob now, and they don't seem to have left a guard of any sort on the airstrip. Come on, it's time for us to go.'

'The last of the mob left hours ago.' Netta was not inclined to forgive him for what she regarded as a totally unnecessary safety margin which Joss insisted on, and which left her frozen to the bone, and more physically wretched than she had ever felt in her life before.

'They might have turned back.' His voice was hard, uncaring for the way she felt. 'I'm responsible for your safety.'

'I'm responsible for myself.' She faced him with what dignity she could muster under the circumstances. 'I'm not....'

'As my wife, you're in my charge,' he reminded her curtly, 'so come with me and don't argue.' He did not leave her enough breath to argue, she thought furiously, he took her along with him willy-nilly, by the same expedient as before. He grasped her wrist and pulled her behind him straight back towards the town.

'Surely you're not going to go back there?' She pulled back fiercely as he made to enter the nearest high-walled alley. 'It's insane!' she protested. 'We should be going the other way, towards the border.' The way the plane went. She tried not to think about the plane.

'We'll make for the border later,' he tugged her remorselessly forward again. 'First, we must have food. Enough to eat now, and enough to take with us. The country between here and the border is desolate, and we can't travel a hundred miles without eating.'

'There must be villages,' she argued.

'Which we will have to avoid,' he told her sharply. Just as he avoided the bands of roaming insurgents who appeared with breath-stopping suddenness out of the darkness ahead and behind them as they crossed the town, until Netta began to despair of them remaining undiscovered. But beyond pausing to draw her into a doorway, or against

a wall now and then, Joss did not stop. With a catlike silence
of tread he followed a route of his own until at last he came
to a halt in what appeared to be the garden of a large
house. The high walls rose out of the darkness ahead of
them, and Netta could distinguish bushes of some kind
grouped together in a small shrubbery. She brushed
against one of them, and the aromatic smell from the
bruised leaves reached her nose in pungent protest at her
carelessness.

'This way.' He forced her right into the middle of the
shrubbery, ignoring the scratching twigs himself, and
obliging her to do the same, until,

'Oh!' She cried out as the ground fell sharply from
beneath her feet and she stumbled forward, knocking
against him.

'Steady,' he admonished her sharply, and set her on her
feet again. 'Look where you're going.'

'How can I look? It's as black as a mineshaft here,' she
flared resentfully.

'You're entering a passageway that runs underground,'
he informed her briefly. 'That's why it slopes away from
your feet. Keep your hands on my waist, and walk behind
me.' He guided her hands to his belt and held them there
with his own, and started forward again with a flat-hipped
stride that made no concession to her own unsteady pro-
gress. She stumbled behind him, incensed by his lack of
consideration, but not daring to let go, not daring to lose
contact with him in the darkness.

'You can loose me now, we've arrived.' He let go of her
hands as the floor flattened out under their feet, and she
reluctantly withdrew them. Contrarily, she did not want to
loose him now. A tingling awareness of him flowed through
her finger ends like molten fire, driven by the wild, uneven beating of her heart. His nearness worked on her
senses with the potency of vintage wine, until the heady
excitement of it made her sway.

'Sit down.' He guided her to a bench of sorts, and she
sat. She brushed a hand across her eyes, trying desperately
to still the clamour of emotion inside her. She resented its

hold on her, but she could not control it, and she took a deep breath, trying to appear normal as he spoke.

'Do you feel faint?' For the first time, a hint of concern for her showed in his voice. He must have taken her plea of hunger seriously, she thought caustically.

'No,' she shook her head, 'it's something in my eye.'

'Let me have your handkerchief, and I'll get it out for you. It's light enough in here to see if you come over to the grating.' She became aware for the first time of daylight filtering through bars somewhere above their heads.

'I thought I had my hanky.' She fumbled in her pocket, reluctant to give it to him, unwilling for him to discover that there was nothing at all the matter with her eye. 'I can't find it,' she discovered. 'I must have dropped it somewhere. It doesn't matter anyhow—whatever it was has gone. It was probably only an inturned eyelash.' She dared not allow him to touch her again, his nearness evoked feelings that she must not allow to show in her face, for fear they betrayed themselves to him. Feelings that she dared not acknowledge, even to herself. . . .

'Do you remember when you had your handkerchief last?' His look was keen, his tone sharp, and his interest in her eye forgotten.

'I don't know.' She wrinkled her forehead. 'I think it was while we lay in the scrub at the side of the airstrip.' She remembered quite distinctly when she last used it, to mop up the tears that she refused to let Joss see. She had not needed it since, and now it was gone. What did a handkerchief matter? 'Where are we?' She dismissed it, and looked about her curiously. They appeared to be in some kind of cellar.

'We're in the safest possible place.' Unexpectedly he grinned. It gave his face a puckish look that took years from his age, and drew her own lips up in a reluctant answering smile. 'We're in the vaults below the Embassy,' he enlightened her.

'What?' She sat up with a suddenness that set the bench underneath her rocking dangerously.

'Shhh! Not so loud,' he cautioned swiftly, and grabbed

the bench in time to prevent it from crashing to the floor.

'I thought you said the Embassy had been evacuated?'
Instinctively she whispered, reacting to his mood. 'I can
hear someone talking.' The sounds came from above their
heads, in what must be one of the ground floor rooms.

'The Embassy staff were evacuated,' he confirmed, 'the
insurgents have taken over the Embassy as their head-
quarters,' he added casually.

'You mean ...?' Shock stopped further utterance, and
she swallowed convulsively. 'You knew that, and you
deliberately came back here? Brought me here?'

'If you can't beat them, join them,' he quipped, then
more seriously, 'This is the last place they'll think to look
for the opposition,' he assured her with beautiful sim-
plicity.

'Opposition?' Her stunned senses latched on to the last
word. 'Surely you're not going to remain here and organise
a resistance?'

'No,' to her relief he shook his head, and his face grew
grave. 'My assignment in Lak has ended.' He spoke without regret. 'Any resistance the insurgents meet must come
via the Lak Government forces. I've finished the job I
came for.'

'What was your job?' She rounded on him suddenly,
goaded out of her desire to appear indifferent to him. 'Who
are you—what are you?' she demanded. 'I've got a right to
know who I married.' The aura of mystery that surrounded
him both intrigued and repelled her, in spite of the fact
that Harry Fraser had vouched for him.

'I came out to Lak at the instigation of their Government and our own, for the sole purpose of making sure the
Lak Royal Family escaped with their lives, in the event
the unrest became an uprising.' He joined her on the bench
and spoke quietly, without emphasis, as if such an assignment was an everyday, unremarkable affair to him. Netta
expected him to argue, perhaps tell her to mind her own
business. To her surprise he did neither, but treated her
demand as if it was an eminently reasonable one.

'The Lak Royal Family?' she breathed, taken aback by

the sheer unexpectedness of his answer. She did not question that he told her the truth. She sensed that with Joss, he would tell the truth or not tell at all. 'No wonder Harry wouldn't talk about you,' she remembered the Ambassador's evasiveness. 'He told me you were one of his aides.'

'It was a useful cover,' Joss conceded, 'and the Frasers were very helpful. But I had ways open to me that were denied the Embassy.'

Secret ways, she thought. 'The ways of a fox?'

'If you like,' he smiled again. 'The people who call me that are not the only ones to see the likeness,' he commented obliquely. 'But I must go,' he rose to his feet abruptly. 'We must have food.'

'Don't leave me here alone.' Her fear rose anew, not of Joss so much now, but of being left on her own. What if he did not come back?

'I'll be back, never fear. Don't move from here until I come.' His voice hardened into sternness, and his steely glance demanded her promise.

'I'll wait.' She hated the submission, but she would not dare to venture on to the streets on her own for a second time. 'How long——?' she began, but Joss was gone. One moment he was standing by her side, the next the vault was empty, except for herself and—she caught her breath as a rustling sound came from the darkness of the far corner, then she relaxed and gave a shaky laugh. 'It's only a rat.' By contrast with the present occupants of the Embassy, a rat could not raise even a tremor in her.

'How will this suit you, for breakfast?'

She did not hear him come back. He reappeared beside her with the same silent step that had taken him away, but this time his arms were loaded, and he handed over his booty with an almost boyish pride.

'A loaf—cheese, meat, cake, fruit—a bottle of wine?' She accepted his treasures with growing wonder. 'Where on earth did you get these from? You must have looted the nearest grocer's shop,' she accused him.

'On the contrary, my foray was quite legal and above

board,' he told her loftily. 'I got them from the Embassy pantry upstairs. As a member of the staff, I've got every right.'

'You shouldn't have taken the risk. What if....' She raised dismayed eyes to his, unable to go on.

'The squatters upstairs don't know all the ins and outs of the building yet,' he quietened her fears. 'They've mainly occupied the downstairs rooms, they haven't had a lot of time to explore. They weren't to know there's an upstairs pantry to serve the banqueting suite. Fortunately, I did,' he grinned. 'Oh, by the way, while I was about it, I purloined one of Wendy's handkerchiefs for you. Don't lose this one,' he warned her, 'I may not be able to get another replacement.'

She took his offering, and tried not to think of the danger he had risked in order to get it for her. 'Come and eat.' She turned to the food, unwilling that he should see her expression. 'You've even brought paper cups.' Her voice wobbled slightly out of control, and Joss gave her a keen glance.

'Let me fill them.' He opened the bottle of wine, and poured.

'Not too much,' she held up a cautionary hand. 'I don't drink wine very often except at Christmas and birthdays. It always makes me feel sleepy.'

She was too late to stop him, or else he did not hear her, because he handed her a paper cup brim full.

'Try it,' he urged when she hesitated, 'it won't hurt you. It's a local wine, and very good.'

Encouraged by Joss, she sipped cautiously. The liquid was sweet, and light, and seemed more like a cordial. Her fears allayed she drank thirstily, and the warm glow of it ran through her, taking away the stiffness and the cold of the night. The food revitalised her flagging energy, and suddenly their impromptu picnic became a feast. Quite how it happened she did not know, but soon she and Joss were talking together as if no antagonism had ever existed between them. True, they kept their voices to a whisper, a necessary concession to the constant tramp of feet across the grating above their heads, that would not allow them to forget their position as refugees, but in spite of the danger, the conspiratorial atmosphere added a spice to the food—to the company....

'Did you manage to get them away in the end? The Lak Royal Family, I mean?' Resolutely she turned her thoughts in another direction, and shook her head at his offer of more food.

'Yes, they all went on the plane along with the Embassy staff.'

The plane that she and Joss should have been on. That they would have been on, if she had remained at the Embassy, as he told her to. If he had not come to find her. If the insurgents had not arrived when they did, and blocked her way back. Joss blamed her, but it was not her fault. She checked her mind again, with another question.

'Will you come back to Lak, afterwards?' She spoke without thinking, as if they were casual acquaintances, as if there was no tie between them. Then she remembered, and her fingers twisted the slender gold ring round and round, nervously, until she caught his glance, watching her, and stopped abruptly. Perhaps he already had a girl waiting for him in England. He would probably start proceedings to have their marriage annulled the moment they reached home, and safety.

'I'm glad,' she told herself fiercely. 'I'll give him his ring back the very moment we dock. I'll be free, the same as before.' But while her mind exulted at the prospect, a small corner of her heart traitorously died within her at the inevitability of it all, at the knowledge that it could never be quite as it had been before, and she had to steel herself to listen when he answered,

'No, I shan't return to Lak. Thimbles needs me now. It's time for the fox to return to his lair,' he said quietly, and smiled, as if he found the prospect good.

'Thimbles?' Surely that was the name of his home. She remembered Wendy telling her. It was an odd sort of name for a home, she thought, and fought down a desire to giggle. Joss might be offended if she laughed at the name of his home. To stop the giggle she picked up her cup and raised it to her lips, then paused with a frown. 'That's funny, it's full!' She could have sworn she had already drunk at least half of her wine.

'Drink it up while I put the rest of the food away for later,' Joss said casually. He did not answer her questioning look, but continued to pack the remains of their meal carefully back into its wrapping. His voice seemed to reach her from a long way away, and when she looked at him his features were curiously blurred. Why did his face look blurred? She blinked, trying to bring it into focus, and was surprised by a yawn.

'I—feel—shleepy....'

'Good,' Joss approved, and turned towards her. 'Don't try to fight against it,' he advised her calmly. 'Just let go.' He caught her in his arms as she attempted to stand, and swayed dizzily. 'The wine will make sure you sleep soundly until I get back,' he said, and there was a wealth of satisfaction in his voice. She felt him wrap her in something warm and soft, it must be a blanket of some kind, and although she struggled to keep on her feet, her arms were pinioned inside its folds, and she was unable to offer any resistance when he picked her up easily and laid her down like a child, and her cheek encountered—surely, one of Wendy's pillows? Joss must have purloined the blanket and pillow on purpose, intending to ply her with the wine until she was drowsy. Through the mists that fogged her mind she realised, dimly, that she had not seen him drink more than sparingly of his own cup.

'This time I'll make sure you stay in the Embassy until I get back,' he said. And he laughed.

Through the drugged drowsiness that clawed her irresistibly into the maw of sleep, her last conscious feeling was one of burning anger against Joss, and the unscrupulous methods he had adopted to bend her to his will. First, he kissed her to keep her quiet. She would never forgive him for that kiss. Never! she vowed. Now he plied her with wine, that he must have known was potent, even if it seemed to her to be mild, until she had drunk deeply, and discovered its treachery—Joss's treachery—too late. Through the growing darkness she heard his laugh, and hated him for it. Desperately she struggled to stay awake, to tell him that she hated him. . . .

She slept.

She awoke to the sound of voices. Someone was close by, talking in low tones. Talking about her. She opened her eyes and stared straight up into the olive-skinned face of a man in the act of bending over to touch her hair. She sat up abruptly, her eyes widening with alarm, and Joss said,

'Don't panic. He's a friend.'

'How was I to know that?' she snapped, anger following on the heels of fright. 'He doesn't wear a label.'

The stranger spoke, to Joss, not to her.

'You would pass all but a close inspection, if you adopted native dress, but the woman would not.'

'Woman, indeed!' Netta spluttered indignantly, and a fleeting grin lightened Joss's face as the stranger continued,

'Her hair would give her away. And so would her temper. Our women are submissive.'

'Well, I'm not!' Netta tossed the blanket aside and gained her feet in one angry movement.

'You see?' The man shrugged helplessly. 'It would help, of course, if her hair was black. I'll bring you dye.'

'Dye my hair? Never!' Netta's hands rose to her head in defence of her copper curls.

'No,' Joss was equally decisive. 'We'll travel by night instead. The darkness will act as a cloak.'

Netta stared at him in surprise. She did not expect him to uphold her. Rather, she thought he would take a perverse pleasure in making her change the colour of her hair. She stiffened, prepared to do battle with him over the issue, and now he left her with nothing to fight against. Deliberately, to provoke her, she felt certain. She let her breath out in a deflated puff, but before she could think of anything to say, another voice joined in the conversation, and a man appeared out of the shadows from the other end of the vault.

'You'll need speed, as well as a cloak, to save you now.'

He gave Netta a peculiar look, and beckoned to the other
two men. 'I wish to speak,' he insisted, and led Joss and his
companion aside, away from Netta.

Really, the men were impossible! All three of them, she
fumed. They treated her as if she was of no account, not
even there, in fact, though it soon became obvious that she
was the subject of their conversation. Several times the last
comer gesticulated fiercely in her direction, and although
the men kept their voices low they appeared to be arguing
among themselves. Netta watched them with growing un-
ease. The two strangers argued in a language she was un-
familiar with, doubtless so that she should not understand
what they said, since they had both spoken to Joss in good
English earlier. He seemed to have no difficulty in understanding them, and joined in the conversation in the same
tongue. She would give a great deal to know what they
were talking about, she thought uneasily, but the tempta-
tion to butt in and demand to know evaporated swiftly
when she glanced at Joss's face.

In response to a particularly violent gesture from the
second of the two men, he turned and looked across at
Netta, and his eyes were flint hard. She caught her breath
sharply. What were the two strangers saying, to make him
look at her like that? His eyes seemed to bore right
through her. And then, just as abruptly, he looked away,
back to the other two men. He shook his head and spoke
sharply to them, stilling whatever argument it was they
were pressing. At first, Netta thought, they looked nonplussed, then the first man shrugged as if giving up, and
without more ado they both melted back into the shadows
towards where the tunnel from the garden led into the
vaults.

'What was that all about?'

She tried to sound casual, but tension showed in her
voice, and in the tautness of her slender figure as she
faced Joss defensively. Defending herself against what she
did not know, unless it was against the cold anger that
hardened his eyes and his expression as he turned to con-
front her, and stood for what seemed endless minutes look-

ing down at her with a close, searching scrutiny that made
her eyes falter nervously under his stare. He noticed them
falter, and an ominous frown darkened his forehead as he
spoke.

'What have you done with the jewels you stole?' he demanded harshly. 'The ones you took from their settings
that you hid in your hotel room?'

CHAPTER FIVE

'THE jewels I stole?' She stared at him, stunned. 'I didn't steal them,' she denied hotly, 'I . . . .'

'Don't lie to me,' he snapped. 'Those two men who've just gone are reliable contacts of mine. The second one who came in brought the news that the mob had raided the hotel, and found a pile of jewel settings—without the jewels,' he stressed harshly. 'The settings were hidden underneath a pile of women's clothing in a guest's bedroom. The guest could only have been you.'

So that was why the newcomer had looked at her in such a peculiar fashion.

'Is that what you were arguing about?'

'I was arguing to prevent them from straightaway handing you over to the authorities to deal with,' he told her bluntly, 'which means, at the moment, the rebels themselves.'

'They can't!' She stared at him, horrified. 'They wouldn't—I thought you said they were contacts of yours?' Surely they could not be in sympathy with the rebels too?

'The jewel settings which the looters found were all traditional to Lak,' Joss reminded her grimly. 'And while the two men you saw here have no sympathy with the uprising, they have even less with foreigners who try to steal their national wealth.'

'I didn't steal them,' she cried angrily. She knew, even better than Joss, what the settings were like. Somehow she must convince him of her right to the jewels, make him convince the two strangers. While they were with him, Joss had prevailed, but once they were out of earshot, away from the influence of his stronger personality, they might have second thoughts about handing her over to the rebels. Fear paralysed her at the very thought. She must

52

not let Joss know where she had hidden the gems. He would undoubtedly force her to hand them over, to buy her safety, and she had promised Ranjit.... Nothing would make her go back on that promise, she vowed stubbornly. Where she went, the jewels would go with her, until they reached the safety of their client's bank in London.

'Well?' Joss took her by the shoulders and gave her a shake, misconstruing her silence. 'Is that why you came to Lak in the first place? Tell me the truth,' he demanded fiercely. 'I've got a right to know who I married, as well as you,' he used her own words against her, 'and I want to know whether or not I've married a....'

'Jewel thief?' She drew herself up proudly. 'You can set your mind at rest on that score,' she assured him coldly. 'And before you decide to act as judge, jury and executioner, you might do me the courtesy of listening to my side of the story.'

'Go on.' His face did not relent, and he kept hold of her by the shoulders still. 'As if I might make off with the loot,' she thought bitterly, and resisted an urge to slide her fingers round her slacks belt to make sure the jewels were still there. With an effort she took control of herself, and went on more quietly,

'You already know who my father is.' There could be few who did not know John Vaughan, at least by reputation, and she blessed the fact now. 'I came to Lak to collect some jewels from a client, to take back with me to be re-modelled.' She mentioned Ranjit's name, and could see from the quick interest on Joss's face that he knew who she meant. 'I often act as a courier between my father and his clients, but this is the first time I've been accused of stealing the jewels I come to collect,' she finished bitterly.

'Are you in the habit of extracting the gems from their settings after you've collected them?' he enquired sarcastically, and she flushed.

'I usually wait until I get them home,' her own voice reflected the bite in his, 'but I'm not usually faced with the prospect of a mob of looting insurgents on the one hand, and a threat of a baggage search by soldiers I don't trust any more than I trust the rebels, on the other,' she retorted with spirit, and had the satisfaction of feeling his fingers lessen their grip on her shoulders. She half put up her hand to rub the place where they had been, it tingled still with the force of his hold, but she refused to allow him to see that it hurt, and resolutely thrust her hand into her slacks pocket instead. 'The gemstones themselves were the really valuable part of the jewellery, and I was responsible for their safety, so I had no option but to hide them. If you want to check my story, you can always ask Ranjit,' she hurried on for fear he might ask her whereabouts she had hidden them. 'He'll vouch for what I say,' she finished triumphantly.

Joss stared down at her for long minutes, his strange gold eyes probing deep into her own, and she met his look without flinching.

'You'll have to leave the gems wherever they are, and risk them being found,' he said at last. 'You can't go back for them now, the rebels will be on the lookout for you to return to the hotel and try to retrieve them.'

'He hasn't guessed!' Relief surged through her. 'He thinks I hid the gemstones in the hotel, as well as the settings.' She lowered her eyes hastily for fear they might reflect her jubilation, and give her away.

'That accounts for the jewels, but it doesn't explain the missing film.'

'What about the film?' She had completely forgotten about it until now. 'At least I've got that with me.' Where did I learn to be devious? she asked herself, astonished, her normally truthful self looking on amazed at the ease with which the inferred lie came out. 'I've got that with me.' Saying without words that she had left the jewels behind. Confirming Joss's supposition that she had done just that. 'It's only holiday snaps I took on safari,' she told him guilelessly. 'You can have the film by all means, if you want it, it's in my bag somewhere.' She bent to get it for him, and he checked her movement with his hand.

'Don't bother, you might need it to convince the authorities if we're unlucky enough to be caught.'

'Why should a holiday film bother them? It wasn't even taken in Lak.' She was genuinely puzzled now, and showed it, and the stern set of his features relaxed a little.

'Only a blameless life could make you so naïve.' The way he said it, it did not sound like a compliment, and she eyed him warily. 'Try and look at it from the point of view of the people who raided your room,' he dropped his hands from her shoulders and spoke with barely controlled patience. 'They found you and the jewels missing, and as if that wasn't enough, they discovered some extremely expensive photographic equipment apparently abandoned without a second thought, and the clip of films was gone. What conclusion could they come to, but that the film was as valuable to you as the jewels?' he asked her impatiently.

'So?' She shrugged, unable to see the point he was driving at.

'Give me patience!'

Joss's plea went unheard, and his own evaporated.

'Can't you see?' he asked her, tensely. 'The stuff you left behind in the hotel not only brands you as a jewel thief, but as a possible spy as well.'

'A spy?' He sounded like a paperback thriller, she thought scornfully. 'You're talking nonsense! If we're unlucky enough to get caught by the rebels, I can easily explain....'

'Do you imagine they'd wait long enough to listen to your explanation?' he interrupted her roughly. 'In the mood the mob's in now, they'd act first and think afterwards.'

'They'll think I've escaped on the plane.'

'They know differently,' he disillusioned her. 'They found your handkerchief in the scrub bordering the airstrip. It was caught on a twig, and waving at them like a flag. They couldn't miss it,' he accused her tersely.

'I didn't leave it there on purpose.' She refused to be pilloried for something else that was not her fault.

'If you had, it couldn't have served as a clearer guide.' He refused to relent. 'It took no time at all for the rebels to put two and two together, and realise you'd missed the plane, and must therefore be still somewhere in Lak.'

'That means. . . .' She stared at him, silenced by the implications of what he had just told her.

'That means the rebels would dearly like to discover where you're hiding.' He did not mince words, and she shivered. 'They'd give a great deal to get their hands on the jewels you hid, and only you're in the position to tell them where they are.'

'What shall we do?' she asked in a dry whisper. Visions of the man with the chain rose frighteningly before her.

'We'll travel by night,' Joss answered briefly. 'Very soon one of my contacts will return with two night cloaks. They'll serve as a disguise enough in the darkness unless we have the ill luck to be actually confronted by someone.'

He did not suggest what they might do then. Netta swallowed. Night cloaks were a good idea, but. . . . She thought longingly of the safety of the aeroplane, and then resolutely thrust the thought aside. It was no good wishing. The ankle-length night cloaks would have to do. They were a reasonable enough disguise, as Joss said, because they were a common article of clothing worn by the Lak people who used them as a simple solution to the problem of the severe variance in temperature between day and night, which fluctuated between sub-tropical at noon and sub-zero after dark, occasioned by the high altitude of the country.

Her own cloak trailed on the floor forlornly when she tried it on. She did not expect the two men to return, but Joss's faith in them proved to be justified, and shortly after dark they came with two bundles of clothing, and left again immediately.

'They haven't. . .?' She raised apprehensive eyes to Joss.

'They won't betray you,' he answered the question she dared not ask. 'Try this on,' he thrust the smaller of the two bundles towards her.

'It's too long.'

'Of course it is, if you wear it across your shoulders. The men wear theirs that way.' He slung his own cloak across his shoulders in a manner that told her he had worn one before, probably for the same purpose, as a disguise. It gave him a brigandy sort of look, she decided critically, and felt her heart begin to thump uncomfortably hard. It made him look even more handsome, if anything.

'The women of Lak keep their heads covered.' He removed her cloak from about her shoulders and draped it across her hair. 'That's better.' He surveyed the length of it critically. 'It's free from the floor, so you can walk without tripping over it. Or run, if you have to,' he added significantly.

'It feels like a nun's habit.'

'You don't look a bit like a nun.'

Unexpectedly he reached out and caught her to him. She raised her head, startled, and the cloak slipped from off her hair, framing her face in its soft woollen folds, and Joss cupped his hands round her head and tipped her face up towards him.

'You weren't meant to be a nun,' he affirmed softly, and lowered his head until his lips trailed lightly across the delicate softness of her cheek. They explored the fine bone line to where a dimple showed at the corner of her mouth when she laughed. She was not laughing now, but he found the spot where the dimple lay with unerring accuracy.

Netta quivered under his touch, and went deathly still. She tried to steel herself against him, valiantly trying not to respond, but her heart hammered against her ribs in a wild tattoo, and the urge to put her arms round his neck became irresistible, until she tried to raise them, and found them trapped beneath the enmeshing folds of the cloak. Joss drew it even more closely round her, and laughed down into her face, enjoying her predicament.

'The cloaks serve more than one useful purpose,' he murmured. 'The Lak men like their women submissive.'

'I'm not a Lak woman,' she denied hotly, stung into anger by his amusement. She hated him, when he laughed at her. 'And I'm not submissive, either.'

'If you hope to pass as a Lak woman, you'll have to learn how.'

His lips left her dimple and sought her mouth. They

parted her lips with a firm pressure that stilled the angry
words they were forming, until the words no longer
wanted to come. She tried in vain to stiffen herself away
from him, terrified by the ease with which he was able to
bend her to his will. Her mind cried out to her to resist, but
her heart treacherously refused her the ability.

'I can't fight you. I can't,' she moaned when at last he
let her go, and she leaned trembling and defeated against
him.

'For your first try at being submissive, that wasn't bad,'
he approved. 'Keep it up, and you'll pass as a Lak woman
yet.'

She recoiled from him as if she had been stung.

'You—you——' she choked into silence on a sob. Once
again he had tricked her into responding to his kisses, playing on her feelings as a harpist plucks the strings of his
instrument, cynically drawing out the notes for his amusement. And she had provided the tune.

'Don't ever touch me again,' she cried fiercely. 'Never,
do you hear me? Never—never. . . .' In a frenzy of anger
she thrust the folds of the cloak from her and raised her
hand to strike him.

'It's time to go.'

Joss fielded her hand neatly and spun them both round
as a voice spoke from the shadows behind them. A figure
stood at the entrance to the tunnel into the shrubbery.

'We're ready.' Joss loosed her hand, contemptuously indifferent to her anger, and the possibility that she might
again attempt to hit him.

'Keep your hair covered,' he commanded her curtly, 'or
it'll betray us both.' For a dreadful second or two she felt
she did not care, until he added, 'jewels aren't worth risking your life for.' His comment stilled her. Had he
guessed? She shook herself mentally. There was no way in
which he could possibly know. But the doubt was sufficient
to keep her still when he turned and pulled her cloak over
her head with an impatient tug, before he put his arm
round her shoulders and swung her with him to join the
man who waited for them. His cloak swirled about him
as he turned, faintly theatrical in the gloom, and it added

to Netta's sense of unreality as she went with him, feeling as if she was taking part in a bizarre play.

'There's no need to pull me along as if I'm on a lead,' she protested angrily, stumbling in her efforts to keep pace with the long strides of the men as they emerged through the shrubbery, and out once more into the dreaded alleyways.

'You must keep up with us,' he said curtly, but just the same he added something in the same strange tongue she had heard him use with the men before, and the one who led them slackened his pace slightly. It was a relief, but Netta still found she had to trot to keep up with them.

'The men of Lak must train their women like racehorses, if this is the pace they expect them to walk at,' she panted resentfully when they paused at the exit from the alley they were traversing, and which emerged, she saw with dismay, on to the central square of the town near to the front of the hotel which had been her recent abode.

'Their women are wise, they remain in their homes,' Joss retorted. Netta scowled at this implied criticism, but before she could reply he went on unsympathetically, 'Only ladies of doubtful virtue venture abroad after dark.' She saw his teeth flash white in the guttering light of the flares that threw a mixture of flame and smoke among the groups of figures, cloaked like themselves, who moved restlessly in the broken darkness around the edges of the square.

'Well, they needn't think that about me,' she whispered, furious at his jibe.

'I hope that's just what they will think if we're unlucky enough to be confronted by any of the rebels,' Joss answered unfeelingly, and raised his hand to their guide in a dismissive gesture.

'What are you signalling to him for?' Netta demanded to know uneasily.

'His job's finished,' Joss told her as the guide turned the corner into the square and mingled unobtrusively with the groups of rebels. 'From now on, we're on our own.'

She despised herself for the thrill his words sent through

her, and conflicting emotions made her voice sharp as she replied fervently,

'I wish we were on our own, miles away from here.' She eyed the knots of cloaked men fearfully. 'We'll have to go some other way. We can't go through that crowd, or we're sure to be discovered. There isn't a woman among them,' she discovered, and checked, appalled. Joss did not just hope what they would think when they saw a woman with him. He had known, before he brought her here.

'I'm not going to cross the square. You can't make me!'

'You must. All roads lead into the square, and the way to the border is on the other side.'

He made her. He caught her by the shoulders as she tried to escape past him, back into the darkness of the alleyway, and propelled her forcibly into the square. A group of rebels strolled towards them, and called out something to her, and ribald laughter rose at whatever it was they said, from others of their kind nearby. Joss snarled something back in the same tongue, and grabbed her roughly to him. One arm went round her waist, the other held the cloak over her head, over her face. She felt trapped, stifled, and something inside her snapped. Throwing caution to the winds, she beat against him with her fists, suddenly terrified, frantic to be free.

'Let me. . . .' She did not get as far as the word 'go'. He silenced her with a kiss of such force that it pressed her lips back against her teeth, bruising, agonisingly painful. Momentarily, shock stilled her. And then a wave of pure fury flooded through her at his brutality. She had warned him not to touch her again, and this was his answer. He was behaving like an animal—a savage! The sheer primitive ferocity of his attack—it could not be called a kiss— goaded her into retaliating.

Unable to speak, because his face pressed down over her own like a mask, she lashed out with her feet and fists, careless now of the rebels around them, fighting like a tigress in a personal rebellion of her own that made the other war seem tame by comparison. Her nails scored deeply across his face, and he jerked his head sharply upwards with a quickly checked curse. Several voices rose from the watching rebels, offering him jeering advice. Netta could not understand the words, but there was no mistaking the tone. She longed to shout back at them, denying that she was what they thought her to be, but her lips were numb with the cruel pressure upon them, and would not form the words.

Without warning, the shouts and jeers grew dim, and she swayed, half fainting. She felt Joss's arm move from behind her waist and grasp her under the knees, and he lifted her bodily, holding her tightly against him so that her face was buried in the folds of his own cloak. He pulled it round her and she lay against him, spent, longing to cry, and yet terrified of making a sound. A confusion of shouts broke out round them, and rough hands grasped at her. She shrank against Joss, too petrified to cry out, and the rumble of his ferocious answering shout resounded through his chest against her ear. He swung round and her feet, sticking out horizontally as he carried her, struck something soft and yielding. He was using her as a club! She risked a peep, and saw the ring of men around them fall back, giving way, and Joss loped through the gap, carrying her easily, as if she was some kind of prey he had fought for and won, and then the shouts died away behind them, and the guttering light and smoke from the flares gave way to blessed darkness. Still Joss travelled on, unspeaking, until at last she felt him slow his pace, and she became conscious of cold; biting cold that gripped her feet where her cloak had fallen away from them. She stirred in his arms and shivered, and Joss stopped and stood her down on the ground, holding her against him for support.

'We're nearly there.'

She was too exhausted to ask where 'there' might be.

'Can you stand?' He hardly waited for her nod. 'Then walk,' he commanded her, 'it'll warm you.' She stumbled, but he forced her to go on. The flow of blood returning to her numbed feet brought pins and needles, and excruciating pain, and the bitter cold of the pre-dawn made her gasp. The ground they were traversing was rough and steep, and thickly dotted with scrub, similar to the perimeter of the airstrip.

'I can't go on.' She sank weakly to her knees.

'Walk!' he commanded her harshly, and pulled her upright again, relentlessly forcing her forward. 'We've got to reach the cave before daylight.'

'Cave?' His callous treatment had the effect he intended. Warmth began to seep through her as he forced her forward. It steadied her shaking limbs, and enabled her to place her feet with greater surety, so that she did not stumble so often.

'It's a hole in the rocks. It runs off the hillside,' he told her briefly. 'The locals know of it, but the rebels won't. The two men you saw at the Embassy have left us more food there, and blankets.'

Blankets. Blessed warmth. The urge to sleep was almost overwhelming, aided by the intense cold. She felt too tired to feel hunger, or even surprise when the thorns of the dense scrub released their clutching hold on her cloak, and they walked free, on rock. Jumbled, tumbled rock, remains of some prehistoric eruption, that received them into its jagged midst, and straightway deprived her of——

'Joss!' Panic caught her as he vanished.

'Follow me.' His arm reappeared round what looked at first glance to be a solid rock face, but upon following his guiding grasp she discovered a fissure just wide enough to allow the passage of her body. She eased herself sideways through the slit, and her feet stumbled on something soft. She put out her arms to save herself, and Joss caught her as she fell.

'They've done us proud!'

He lowered her on to the pile of dark blankets on the cave floor, and she looked up, dazedly surprised that she could see his face clearly.

'It's light!' she exclaimed.

'We've made it just in time.'

The sun rose with the same abruptness with which it had set the night before. One moment they were groping in darkness, the next, it was broad daylight.

'Your face is bleeding,' Netta realised.

'From where you scratched me.'

He reached up slim brown fingers and traced the score lines across his cheek. He slanted a look at her across the heap of blankets, and latent anger glowed deep in the gold eyes.

'You're an excellent actress,' he congratulated her icily, 'but you needn't have made your performance quite so realistic.' His look, his tone, told her she would pay for her temerity.

'My performance?' She gasped at his effrontery. 'What about your own?' she flared angrily. The scratches she had put on his cheek—the thought that it was her nails that had inflicted them made her feel sick—were as nothing to the weals his own play-acting had scored across her heart, not once, but several times.

'I had to silence you somehow,' he shrugged her accusation aside. 'You cried out in English.'

'And that's the best way you know, to silence a woman!' she threw his own taunt back at him with bitter emphasis.

'It worked,' he pointed out irrefutably. 'I wouldn't have bothered, otherwise,' he added in a hard voice, and Netta flinched as if he had struck her. She loathed him, she told herself fiercely, so she did not care. But she could not help the fact that she was feminine enough to feel his indifference as an insult.

'First food, and then sleep.' Joss bent his mind to what he obviously considered more important. How like a man, she thought bitingly.

'I'm not hungry.' She refused the proffered food.

'Nevertheless, you will eat.' He pressed the flat dark bread and strangely spiced meat into her hands, and she ate, reluctantly, but too weary to defy him further, until at last, satisfied, he relented, and spread the blankets flat across what appeared to be a deep bed of twigs on the farther side of the cave floor.

'Are there thorns?' She carried smarting evidence on her legs and hands of the variety carried by the scrub outside.

'No, these are rushes from the river banks just beyond

the cave.' He held the top blanket back, waiting for her to settle herself on the makeshift bed.

'Where are you going to sleep?' Belated compunction caught up with her, and she raised questioning eyes from her couch, which to her surprise felt remarkably comfortable.

'With you, of course.' He watched her eyes widen with startled dismay, and added impatiently, 'It's quite in order. We're married—remember?'

CHAPTER SIX

THE smell of smoke wakened her.

She could not believe that she had slept. She did not think it was possible, when Joss lowered himself on to the rush bed beside her, that she could hope to sleep. She shrank as far away from him as the limited space would allow, and drew her cloak closely, defensively, around her, and felt his look pierce through her like a knife. To avoid it, she turned on her side, away from him, only to discover that it bored through her back until it felt as if it must surely burn a hole through her spine. She lay tense and rigid as he drew the rough woollen blanket over them both and lay down beside her, but he made no attempt to touch her, no attempt to bridge the gap which she put between them by rolling on her side away from him, and she felt unaccountably resentful when, a few minutes later, his even breathing told her he slept.

Sleep seemed far away from Netta, the turmoil of her mind denied that she could ever rest again, but without her being conscious of it, exhaustion took its toll, and the warmth emanating from the blankets and Joss's close proximity to her had their effect, and unaware, she surrendered to oblivion.

The smoke made her cough. It swirled through the cave in thickening clouds, smarting her eyes into tears, and her rested body into alarmed activity.

'Joss, wake up!' She turned and sat up, and discovered the place beside her was unoccupied. She looked round wildly.

'I'm here.' He spoke softly from beside the narrow entrance in the rock. She could just make out his figure in the choking gloom.

'Get out, quick, before we're trapped!' Terror urged her to his side, and the entrance, with the promise of clean air outside the cave.

'The fire's outside, not in here.' He caught and held her back, pulling her to one side of the gap in the rocks.

'But. . . .' She struggled to be free.

'Look outside.' He shook her roughly to make her comply, and retained his tight hold on her jacket, preventing her from moving away from him.

'What are they doing?' Reluctantly she obeyed. It was becoming difficult to breathe, and she held her handkerchief—Wendy's handkerchief, the one he had taken such a risk to obtain for her—over her nose and mouth. Men's figures moved among the smoke outside, and flames crackled hungrily through the wide sweep of tinder-dry thorn and scrub visible from their vantage point among the rocks.

'We've got to get out. We'll be trapped!' It was obvious the unknown men were fighting a losing battle. The whole area appeared to be ablaze, and it was evident that it was beyond the powers of the twenty or so men outside to control it.

'Stay where you are,' he ordered her curtly.

'I can't,' she choked. 'I can't breathe.'

'If it gets more than you can bear, lie face downwards on the floor. Smoke rises, and there'll be an inch or two of clear air at ground level. You can breathe from that.' Joss remained standing himself, his eyes on the activities of the men outside.

'They're not much good at fire-fighting. They're making it worse.' She remained upright as well, unwilling to give in unless Joss did. Unwilling to show weakness in front of him.

'They're not trying to put out the flames. They're deliberately fanning them, to make them spread.'

'But why?' she asked, bewildered. She had seen farmers fire the stubble fields after the harvest in England, but there seemed no point in this. The fire was consuming growing bushes. 'Oh, look, the poor thing's terrified!' she exclaimed pityingly, as a small gazelle-like creature darted out of the scrub, fleeing for its life from the flames.

'That's what they're hoping to do to us—flush us out of

hiding,' Joss told her grimly. 'They must think we're lying out in the scrub somewhere. And they want those gems you hid.' He ignored her involuntary gasp, and went on, 'They can't have found them yet, or they wouldn't be doing this now,' he deduced.

The rebels were a lot closer to the gems than they realised. Instinctively her fingers found her slacks belt, and she checked herself sharply. Joss must not guess, either.

'They're coming closer.' Netta eyed the approaching men uneasily. They had formed themselves into a line, like beaters, and were fanning the flames in front of them, aided by the prevailing wind which blew the smoke away from them, and straight towards the cave.

'They can't know about the cave, otherwise they'd have investigated it before they set fire to the scrub,' Joss returned confidently.

'They might discover it by chance, if they cross the rocks.' She refused to be reassured, and the knowledge of what she carried in her slacks belt added to her anxiety.

'With a bit of luck they'll go round the outcrop of rock,' Joss replied. 'It's cool enough in here, but the sun's hot out there, and the fire will make them hotter still. The rocks make for rough walking, and they're more likely to take the easier route round them. Providing we keep quiet, we stand a good chance of remaining undiscovered,' he added, and his tone held a warning. Twice he had taken drastic measures to silence her.

'I'll be quiet, don't worry,' Netta assured him in a bitter whisper, and anger flared in her as she saw his lips twitch. Resolutely she swallowed a cough as she took her handkerchief from in front of her face for a second or two to brush away an outbreak of irritating tickles that persisted against her neck and arms. It could not be perspiration, in spite of the smoke the cave felt uncomfortably cold, and she had jettisoned her cloak when she rose.

'Ugh!' she muttered.

'Sssh!'

'I can't help it. It's a huge spider,' she whispered back angrily, and brushed it aside with shuddering aversion.

'And another. They must have come from the rushes.'
She regarded the insects with horror. 'No, they're coming
from the roof,' she realised as a dark blob scurried across
her shoulder, and she raised her eyes in shrinking disbelief.
'There's hundreds of them!' Spiders were dropping from
the cave roof; swinging down on webs; crawling down
the walls; doing, in fact, what Joss had told her to do,
seeking the few inches of clear air on the cave floor as the
smoke thickened and rose, and made their shadowy
habitat untenable. 'Great heavens! There's an army of the
creatures!'

A monster of a size and hairiness such as she had never
seen even in her wildest nightmares dropped on the end
of its web, and swung in front of Netta's face like a black,
leggy pendulum. She opened her mouth to scream.

'Quiet!'

Joss's hand clamped over her face with desperate speed,
stifling her cry before it was uttered. His other hand tossed
aside the spider with a savage thrust, and a careless indifference to its horrific appearance that even in extremis,
Netta could not help but envy.

'The spiders won't hurt you. They're not the poisonous
kind.'

She could not care less whether they were poisonous or
not, their looks were enough for her, but with an immense
effort of will she remained silent when at last he removed
his hand from over her mouth with slow caution. When he
was satisfied she would stay quiet he picked her up in his
arms, away from the crawling activity on the cave floor,
and she shuddered, and buried her face in his shirt. With
careful steps he carried her across to the rush bed, and
held her high with one arm while he reached down with his
hand and shook the blankets, ridding them of any stray
spiders that might be lurking there.

'Forget the spiders,' he whispered in her ear. 'Forget the
smoke.' He lowered her gently down on to the rush couch,
and drew the blanket over her, over them both. 'Soon, very
soon, all this will be over, and you can forget,' he promised
her softly, with an un-Joss-like tenderness that made her

wonder if she was dreaming. His lips stopped speaking, and started to blot out the memory for her there and then. Not cruelly, as they had done before, but gently caressing, pressing on her eyelids to shut them against the spiders, wandering from there to the tiptilted end of her nose to tell it not to smell the smoke, trailing rapture behind them as they slowly found their way to the spot where her dimple lay, and lingered there until it deepened into a smile, and then coaxed the hesitant smile into tender, lovely life.

With a sigh she surrendered to his arms, giving herself up to his caress, returning it as it grew urgent, compelling, sweeping her away with an upsurging passion so over-whelming that it was beyond her power to control. It blotted out the danger that threatened them from the rebels outside; drew a veil across the past, and the future, and lit her whole being with a fire that paled the brush fire outside into insignificance by comparison, an all-consuming flame of ecstasy that burned like lightning, and that for the rest of her days would endow the stark cave with a secret beauty of its own, known only to her—and to Joss.

She was alone when she woke up. She looked round her warily, but there was no sign of the spiders. The smoke had vanished, and the insects had retreated to their preferred haunts in the crannies of the cave roof. Netta brushed a hand across her face, clearing her hair from her eyes, and her palm came away showing a black sooty streak.

'I feel filthy!' she groaned.

The smoke had dispersed, but it had left behind marks of its presence in a rash of sooty smudges over her clothes and person, and her thoughts turned longingly towards hot water, and delicately perfumed soap.

She tossed aside the blankets, and stretched. Joss was gone, but he would not be far away. The euphoria of last night remained with her still, boosting her confidence. Everything seemed different this morning. Life itself was different, after last night. She rose to her feet, feeling sur-prisingly refreshed, and blessed the rushes for their hospitality. Tonight, she and Joss would be gone. She bent automatically to fold the blankets in a neat pile, baring the dry, reedy stems of their makeshift bed, and paused, struck by a sudden thought.

Rushes. That meant water. Joss said they had been gathered from a river bank close by. Perhaps that was where he had gone now, maybe to have a swim. The rebels must have departed, for him to risk such a thing. The prospect of cool water, even without soap, proved irresistible. She left the blankets and slid through the slit in the rock, and took a cautious look out over the surrounding terrain. The rebels had indeed gone. There was no sign of human life on the burned-out slopes. The arsonists had unwittingly done her a good turn, in that their vandalism had left them with no place to hide themselves. All that remained of the growing thorn bushes was charred and blackened stumps, incapable of concealing a rabbit, let alone a person. She turned and looked in the other direction. The same black desolation met her eyes, but beyond it the river gleamed, coolly inviting. She hesitated no longer.

'I shan't be away for very long,' she excused her conscience for not waiting for Joss to come back. He could hardly shout at her for leaving the cave on the same errand as himself, she consoled herself. She could not see him by the river, but perhaps he was swimming further along the watercourse.

'I need a wash more than ever now.' She surveyed her feet and legs ruefully as she neared the bank. The charred remains of the scrub had seeped into her shoes on the way, and blackened her slacks as high as her knees, and even without the scrubby thorn growth to contend with, the walking was rough. The day was far advanced, but the sun was still intensely hot, and perspiration streaked her face and stuck her hair damply to her forehead, and she gained the bank with a gasp of relief. It turned into a groan of disappointment as her eyes took in what from a distance had looked to be cool, inviting water.

'Surely Joss isn't swimming in that?' she muttered incredulously. The slow-moving river was an uninviting,

dirty yellow colour, more nearly resembling thick soup
than the clear, bright streams of home, its surface mar-
red by an unidentifiable collection of debris that jostled for
room in the opaque water.

'I'll just damp my hanky, and sponge my face and
hands,' she decided. A side eddy made a patch of clearer
water near to the bank. It was flanked by a strip of dried
mud, punctuated by deep holes that looked as if they had
been made by the hooves of animals. She remembered the
gazelle. She had probably stumbled on the favourite
watering place of the local fauna. She saw Joss in the
distance as she stepped to the edge of the mud patch.

'Netta, don't. . . .'

'Netta, *do*,' she contradicted him crossly as his shout
reached her. The rest of what he said drifted away, and she
set her lips mutinously. Being with Joss was worse than
being at school, she decided, heat and discomfort making
her irritable. Whatever she wanted to do, he seemed to
find a good reason why she should not. 'I'm not a child, and
the sooner Joss realises it the better,' she said to herself
rebelliously, and stepped forward deliberately, ignoring
his second shout. 'If he yells like that, all the rebels in the
state will know we're here—oh!'

Without warning the deceptively firm-looking crust on
top of the mud bank gave way beneath her feet. Black, evil-
smelling slime welled over the tops of her shoes.

'Joss!'

Frantically she tried to backstep, but the mud gave her
no firm footing, and she sank even deeper.

'Joss!'

'Keep still! Don't struggle!' Through a haze of panic
she heard him shout, heard his feet thunder along the sun-
baked earth towards her. He caught her flailing hands in a
firm grasp, and pulled. With a reluctant squelch the mud
released her, and she blessed the fact that her shoes were
sturdy lace-ups. They remained on her feet. She staggered
off balance, unable to keep her footing because of the layer
of mud adhering to the soles, and she scuffed her shoes
hard on the ground to try and clear it.

Joss grabbed her by the shoulders, and stood her on her feet none too gently. 'Didn't you hear me shout?' he demanded angrily. 'I told you not to....'

'I'm not obliged to do as you tell me,' she retorted angrily. If they were going to have a showdown, it might as well be now, she decided. 'I'm an adult, not a child, and I won't be ordered about by you!' she stormed defiantly. It was a pity he towered so far above her, having to look up at him took away some of the force from her defiance, but it was not something she could alter. 'I'm tired of the whole business,' she exclaimed. 'First I get a plague of spiders down my neck, and now I've got fish in my socks!' Exasperation overcame her as she shook a thin, silver, eel-like creature from the inside of her shoe.

'Fish? Where?' Joss stopped glowering, and bent swiftly to grab her foot. Without ceremony he snatched the one shoe from her hand, and swinging her off the floor he tugged her other shoe from her foot.

'There's no need to undress me!' She grabbed back her shoes angrily. 'It's only one small fish.' She had no aversion to fish, only to spiders. 'I'll put it back in the river, it's still alive, if that's what's worrying you.' Really, you could take concern for the environment too far, she thought impatiently, and bent to pick up the wriggling silver body.

'Put it down,' Joss ordered her urgently. 'Drop it!' he shouted when she did not immediately comply, and without waiting to see if his order was obeyed he brushed it from out of her fingers with a hard hand.

'Don't shout at me like that!' She turned on him stormily.

'——!' He swore sharply, and shook his hand violently, ignoring her indignation. For a brief second the creature seemed to cling to his fingers, then with a further violent shake Joss dislodged it, and it described a bright arc and landed back in its own element with hardly a splash.

'It's bitten me!' His face turned colour underneath its tan, and Netta stared at him in surprise. Men were peculiar. The bigger and tougher they were, the bigger babies they seemed to be, she thought scornfully.

'It's nothing to make a fuss about. Good heavens,' she exclaimed, 'the fish isn't as big as a minnow.' She laughed derisively.

'Its bite's deadly poisonous.' He wiped the smile from her face abruptly. 'Help me to pull the heads from these rushes.' He reached out and hurriedly bent the tall stems from across the firm part of the bank, and began snapping off the feathery heads with frantic haste.

'What do you want rush heads for?' Had he gone mad? she wondered impatiently. 'Let me look at that bite,' she insisted.

'There's no time.' He split open one of the rush heads and rubbed it with desperate speed across the place where the creature had bitten him. Netta saw with dismay that his hand was already beginning to turn purple round the bite, and swelling alarmingly. 'The sap contains an antidote,' he explained his actions tersely.

She needed no second bidding to help him. She tore at the rush heads with shaking fingers. The tough fibres of them split her nails, and the juice stained her hands almost as brown as Joss's own, but she did not care. It was her fault he had been bitten in the first place. If only she'd listened. . . .

'I didn't know.' Her whisper begged his forgiveness.

'I shouted, to try and stop you from getting near the water.'

'It looked like an animals' watering place. I thought if the wild things went there to drink, it must be safe.'

'The animals are safe. The fish can't bite through the horns of their hooves, or penetrate the tough hairs on their legs. People haven't got that kind of protection.'

The rapidly spreading swelling along his arm underlined the truth of what he said, and Netta pulled at the rush heads with the speed of fear.

'Help me back to the cave,' Joss said at last, in a breathless kind of voice, and she turned to him sharply.

Help him? An icicle of terror speared through her, and her eyes searched his face. It had gone grey, and—was it her imagination, or did his voice sound slurred? Hurriedly she stuffed a handful of rush heads into her jacket pocket and grasped him round the waist.

'Lean on me,' she bade him, and immediately felt terrified when he did. Joss, who was so strong, who took charge of everything. And now he leaned on her. The slope back to the cave was steep, the going underfoot rough, and Joss's weight was almost more than her slender frame could bear. Rivulets of perspiration stuck her clothes to her body in a clammy embrace.

'If only I'd listened! If only I'd done as he said.' Remorse propped up her flagging reserves of energy when she felt as if her legs must surely give way under her, and she staggered the last few yards to the cave mouth and almost lifted Joss through the entrance as he slumped, barely conscious, in her hold.

'Did you see anyone....' His blurring mind still ran on the rebels.

'No, the slopes are empty.' She searched them with desperate eyes, willing someone to be there. She would even welcome the insurgents, if only they would bring medical aid to Joss. But the blackened terrain surrounding their hideout offered her no support. Even the gazelle had gone.

Somehow she managed to keep upright until they reached the rush bed, and the blankets she had started to fold earlier. The lower one still remained in place, covering the rushes, and she sank on to it on her knees, and lowered Joss down as gently as she could. He collapsed in a limp heap, his eyes half closed, and with a supreme effort she managed to roll him on his back, and pulled the top blanket closely round him. The rush heads dropped from her pocket as she tucked it under him.

'Give me your hand.'

She doubted if he heard her. His eyes were half open, and looked vaguely in her direction, but they had a glazed appearance, as if he did not really see her, their clear bright gold as dull as the waters of the river.

'Stay....' he muttered.

'I'll stay with you, don't worry.' She had no intention

of leaving him. For the first time, she thought wryly, she intended to obey his orders even before they were uttered. She sat back on her heels and hurriedly split open the extra supply of rush heads. If the sap contained an antidote to the poison, then more of the same thing could do nothing but good, she reasoned.

Throughout the endless night she massaged his arm with the brown juice pressing it into the site of the bite, and all the while Joss tossed restlessly on his makeshift bed, muttering with ever rising fever.

At first Netta did not comprehend the words, she was too busy with the rush heads to listen closely to what he said, but in the end the persistent mutter penetrated the daze of exhaustion that, as the long hours passed, turned her movements into automatic reflexes, dictated by subconscious reaction rather than by conscious thought, and she sat back on her heels and listened more closely. Perhaps he wanted something, was trying to tell her to do something for him. She ran out of rush heads, but by now his arm, and the site of the bite, were dyed almost black with their juice, and it was doubtful if more would help.

'Tara . . . stay. . . .'

He shook with cold, and she cradled him to her, holding him in her arms, lying beside him in a vain attempt to warm him with the warmth from her own body. Then the heat of the fever burned him, and he tried to throw off the blanket, and she strained to hold it round him for fear that the cold would return. And all the time he tossed restlessly, calling in delirium for,

'Tara . . . Tara . . . stay. . . .'

She knitted her forehead in a frown. Who was Tara?

When he first begged, 'Stay,' she thought he meant herself; thought he wanted her to remain with him, to help him. Desolation washed over her in a cold wave. It was not her, Netta, Joss wanted at all. It was the unknown Tara.

The name sounded Irish. Visions rose to taunt her, of a black-haired, black-eyed colleen, a lissom fair-skinned girl, endowed with the loveliness born of clear cool air, and the soft benediction of gentle rain.

'Tara . . . stay. . . .'

Why had she left him in the first place? Netta wondered dully. Wondered how she could, ignoring the fact that until last night she herself wanted to do the same. But not since last night. Impulsively she pressed her lips to his unconscious mouth, striving to stop the persistent entreaty that pierced her like a knife; striving to make him recognise her own presence beside him, and forget his need for the other girl.

'Joss, it's me, Netta. I'll stay with you. I won't leave you.'

'I'm jealous,' she acknowledged, but without surprise or shame. She felt she hated the unknown Tara, almost as much as she first hated Joss. As fiercely, she realised, as she now loved him.

'I'll stay with you.' She stroked his hair back from his damp forehead. 'I'll never leave you. Never.'

'Tara ... stay....'

He could not hear her. He did not want her. He only wanted Tara.

'Joss, I love you.' Sudden tears scalded her eyes, cascaded down her cheeks. She pressed her face against his unresponsive lips, that only called for someone else. Willing him to recognise her—to want her....

'Joss, I'm your wife.' The gold of the ring on her finger, the ring that such a short while ago had rested on his, gleamed a silent mockery of her anguish. 'I'm your wife in every way, now,' she whispered, and her trembling lips suddenly firmed in a determined line. 'Nothing can alter that. Nothing—and nobody—will.' Not even the absent Tara, she vowed to herself. Not even she could undo what had passed between herself and Joss, last night.

Unless....

Sudden icy doubt pierced her heart, until it felt as if the pain must surely stop it from beating. Unless Joss had made love to her, simply in order to force her to forget the spiders and the smoke.

Simply—once again—to keep her quiet.

CHAPTER SEVEN

'WHO'S Tara?'

She had not meant to ask him. She spent the night torn between doubt, uncertainty, and a white-hot rage that built up inside her to frightening proportions, so that she alternately longed to strike out at Joss and at the unknown girl he was begging to stay. At last she came to a decision as daylight penetrated the gloom of the cave, and told herself resolutely,

'I won't ask him. I won't let him know I'm even interested. As soon as we reach England I'll give him his ring back, and we'll go our different ways. He can have his Tara, and I'll be free.'

And then, after what seemed a lifetime of agony until the sap from the rushes began its healing work, and Joss at last stopped tossing and calling, and dropped into a deep, natural sleep, and at daylight opened clear eyes that recognised her again, she was unable to stop herself, and straight away blurted out,

'Who's Tara?'

She could have bitten off her tongue the moment the words were uttered, but it was too late to retract now. Joss's hearing, as well as his sight, was restored to normal. He turned his head and looked up at her with a bright, alert gaze, and asked interestedly,

'What do you know about Tara?'

'Nothing,' she responded shortly, and when he continued to look at her, his eyes probing, curious, probably guessing, she added reluctantly,

'You were lightheaded last night, and you kept calling for Tara—whoever she is.' She shrugged, and turned away, and tried to appear indifferent, tried not to see the sudden comprehension, and then the dawning amusement in his eyes as he replied unexpectedly,

77

'You've both got the same coloured hair, you and Tara. Only hers is flat, and yours is curly.'

'Flat? You mean straight, I suppose?'

'Something like that.' He grinned suddenly, and his eyes lit up with a mischievous light. 'It's the same thing.'

'It probably is, to a man.' She cast him a withering look. 'Flat!' she ejaculated scornfully, and turned away so that he should not notice how her lips suddenly trembled, moved out of control by a vision of a regal beauty with straight auburn hair piled high....

'You must have some food. You'll need your strength for when we travel.' She fumbled with fingers that shook at the leather pouch that contained the rest of the food that Joss had purloined from the Embassy kitchen.

'We travel tonight,' he told her.

'You can't be serious?' She spun round in protest, the vision thrust aside by shock. 'You won't be fit enough by tonight to even think of travelling.'

'Fit or unfit, we travel tonight,' he insisted. He pushed himself upright on the rush bed and ran a hand through his hair, rumpling it into wild disorder round his head.

'You can't possibly walk after a fever like that,' she cried. 'At least leave it for another twenty-four hours. The rebels don't know we're here, and we've got enough food to last us if we're careful.'

'We can't leave it,' he told her flatly. 'And I shan't need to walk far, only to the river bank.'

'Not there? Not again!' Netta shuddered.

'We travel by water.' Joss was as unmoved by her aversion as he seemed to be by his own unpleasant experience on the river bank. 'The rush-cutters come with skiffs once a week, and tonight is their night. If we miss it, we'll have to wait another week, and we daren't risk that.'

'Surely men don't cut rushes from the river, and risk being bitten by those awful fish?' She raised a disbelieving face to his.

'That's why they have to come by night,' Joss explained patiently. 'During the hours of darkness, the fish burrow deep into the mud to escape the cold after sundown, so that the river is safe until daylight.'

Even so, Netta's heart thumped uncomfortably against her ribs as she picked her way cautiously downhill beside Joss towards where smoking flares outlined a scene of purposeful activity on the river banks, as the rush-cutters worked methodically felling and loading the rushes into the long, shallow draft boats lined up against the bank.

'What if the rebels are there, among the rush-cutters?' she whispered nervously.

'We should have been warned, if they were,' Joss assured her quietly. 'Keep your cloak over your head, and remember to walk a few paces behind me.' His teeth flashed in a quick grin as he said it, and she retorted waspishly,

'You needn't rub it in! The Lak women are submissive....'

'They know better than to answer back when their menfolk speak,' Joss returned, 'so whatever happens,' he warned, 'keep quiet.' His voice was a command, and Netta subsided into resentful silence. Joss lengthened his stride, which automatically put her in the desired position of a few paces behind him, since her shorter legs could not keep up, and she muttered furiously to herself as she trotted in his wake.

He turned. He must have caught her mutter, and he sent her a quelling glance as a figure cloaked in a similar manner to themselves detached himself from among the rush-cutters on the river bank, and came towards them. Netta stifled a gasp. A machete gleamed wickedly in the stranger's hand. A tool—or a weapon? She froze, and then Joss spoke, using the same strange tongue with which he had addressed the men who came to see him at the Embassy. The stranger replied in kind, and Joss instructed Netta over his shoulder,

'Follow me.'

He did not bother to turn round as he said it. And he did not bother to say 'please'. Netta glared at his tall, retreating back. Arrogant back. She fumed, silently, but she had to follow him. There was no option. It was either do

as he bade her, or be left behind, and the possibility of a
further encounter with the silver fish was even more
daunting than the thought of meeting the rebels.

With one hand she pulled her cloak over her hair and
face, and her other fumbled with her slacks belt. The gemstones felt as large as boulders under her nervous fingers,
and her heightened imagination made them glitter even
through the layers of enshrouding cloth. Cloaked figures
were all around them, but to Netta's relief they took little
notice of either Joss or herself, being too intent on cutting
as many rushes as possible and layering them in the
bottoms of their boats drawn up close against the river
bank.

Their guide gestured to them, and approached one of
the skiffs that had as yet no rushes in it. Without pausing
Joss murmured something to him in a low voice, then
stepped straight off the edge of the bank and into the boat
—and lay down flat in the bottom. Netta stared at him
nonplussed. Had the fever made him so very weak? she
wondered, dismayed. He had shown no sign of lack of
strength while he was walking from the cave, and the
track was rough, even if it was downhill.

'Follow me.' His firm injunction was reassuring, but
what he asked her to do was not. She eyed the gap between
the bank and the boat with growing trepidation.

'I c-can't!' Deep shadows thrown by the guttering light
of the rush-cutters' flares made the extent of the gap in-
distinct. What if she misjudged the distance, and stepped
into the river? What if the light from the flares brought
those terrible fish to the surface, misled into thinking it
was no longer night? Her legs were shorter than Joss's,
and felt distinctly unsure of themselves. It was easy enough
for him to straddle the gap, she thought angrily as she
teetered nervously at the very edge of the water.

'Come on!' His voice from the boat waxed impatient.
'What are you waiting for?'

'I'm waiting for you to help me in,' she whispered
furiously. 'Any gentleman would....'

'The Laks don't behave like gentlemen to women who

wander abroad at night. They're expected to look after themselves.'

'You...!' Sheer fury goaded her into action. 'How dare you!' she breathed, and took a quick, angry step. Too late, she realised that she was stepping over water, that the boat was farther away than she had imagined. 'Help!' Desperately she tried to lengthen her stride in mid-air. She would never make it. She would fall in. The fish.... A hand came out of the bottom of the boat—Joss's hand. It grasped her foot and pulled. Another hand thrust hard against the small of her back, and she fell forward in an undignified heap, and landed in the bottom of the boat on top of Joss. She tried to struggle up, and hard arms went round her and pulled her down beside him.

'Lie still!' he hissed urgently, and pulled her close against him, tugging her cloak over her face and head.

'Let me go!' She started to struggle. 'They'll smother us!' Her voice rose as a shower of rushes descended on top of them.

'Be quiet,' he commanded her harshly. 'They're covering us over, to hide us.'

The sense of what he said penetrated her daze of panic, and with a beating heart she lay tense, but still, in his arms.

'You could have helped me into the boat,' she whispered resentfully when at last the shower of rushes stopped, and he whispered back against her ear,

'If I'd treated you any differently, it would have caused immediate comment, and might have betrayed us. The rebels would love to know where you hid those gems,' he reminded her grimly.

'You said there weren't any rebels among the rush-cutters, otherwise we'd have been warned,' she responded sharply, still smarting from his cavalier treatment.

'So far as we know there aren't, but there might be an informer among them,' Joss replied. 'It's a risk we daren't take, so lie still, and *keep quiet*.'

'There's something sharp digging in my ribs.' She tried to wriggle to a more comfortable position.

'Whatever it is, its better than a gun barrel,' he said

unfeelingly, and she winced into silence as yet more rushes descended on top of them.

'It's a good job they're rushes, and not anything heavier,' was her last conscious thought before, unbelievably, she slept. It might have been the aftermath of the sleepless night before, or the result of strain and fright, or just the gentle rocking of the boat on the slow-moving waters of the river, that lulled her into slumber. Or it could have been the warm, safe feeling, of lying in Joss's arms. . . .

She opened her eyes, and for a wild moment thought she was back in her student days, lying in a punt on the Isis, with her latest admirer poling. Something soft lay under her head, and whatever it was that had stuck in her ribs didn't any more. She sat up and surveyed her surroundings. Nothing could be further from the cool green trees and daisy-starred banks of the Oxford stream. Barren, rocky landscape greeted her from either bank, and in front. . . .

'It's the sea?'

'Not quite,' Joss replied. 'We're approaching the mouth of the river, though, the sea lies a mile or two further on.' He continued to pole, his bare arms flexing with a whip-cord ripple of hard muscle that proclaimed him to be far from the days of callow studenthood.

'It's daylight,' she realised, her fear returning. 'We must find somewhere to hide. I can see boats ahead of us.' That meant people.

She glanced nervously at the distant activity on the rapidly widening watercourse. To get so far, and be discovered now, would be the last straw.

'Relax,' Joss bade her. 'We crossed the Lak border during the night. We're out of danger of pursuit now.'

'You mean . . . but the border was. . . .' The way the plane went, the border was a hundred miles away. Surely Joss could not have poled them so far during one night? And after a bout of fever, the night before? She stared at him with something approaching awe.

'We've come about fifty miles in all, the waterway takes

a short cut through swamp land where the roads can't go,'
he offered her the information laconically.

'Just the same, fifty miles. . . .' She found it hard to grasp
that he could even contemplate getting the skiff so far in
one night. 'You should have rested,' she began, and then
looking at him she realised it was ridiculous to suggest
that he should rest. His easy balance, the lithe sway of his
body as he wielded the long pole and drove the skiff with
sure speed and tireless energy, made rest the last thing he
would contemplate.

'One of the rush-cutters poled us for the first mile or
two.'

She looked down, and saw that the rushes were under
her now, not on top, and they were covered by a cloak—
Joss's cloak; her own was still wrapped round her, carefully tucked in to keep her warm during the long night on
the river, and Joss had kept himself warm by poling the
skiff. She watched him curiously. He was a strange mixture
of harshness and gentleness, this man they called the Fox.
This man who was her husband. . . . First of all he had refused to help her into the boat. Although his reason was for
the sake of their own safety, illogically she still resented his
lack of chivalry. And afterwards, he had stopped to make
her a comfortable bed while she slept, covering the rushes
with his own cloak, and deprived of its warmth himself,
poled them fifty miles across the Lak border to the coast.

'The current helped a lot, fortunately it was going the
same way that we were,' he made light of his efforts with
a shrug.

Which way were they going? she wondered suddenly—
bleakly. She and Joss? She looked up at him, searching his
face, trying to probe the thoughts that lay behind those
strange, gold-coloured eyes. Were they perhaps of England
—and Tara? And maybe the means by which he might
most easily rid himself of a marriage of convenience to
one girl with hair that was auburn and curly, in order to
marry another with hair that was auburn and straight? Flat,
he called it.

Since she intended to return his ring—looked forward to

returning it, she told herself fiercely—it should not matter what he was thinking. Or of whom.

So why should her heart whisper entreatingly of ways by which, if only she wanted to, she might continue to wear Joss's ring? Might make him *want* her to wear it?

CHAPTER EIGHT

NETTA was seasick during the voyage home.

After their traumatic flight from Lak, it was almost ridiculously easy to obtain a berth when they at last reached the docks. In spite of their disreputable appearance and total lack of luggage, Joss's name once more seemed to work some kind of magic, and it seemed to Netta they had no sooner found the shipping agents than they were on board a vessel, and heading on the long trek towards England. True, it was not a palatial liner.

'It's a cargo vessel, with limited passenger accommodation,' Joss told her when he rejoined her outside the shipping agents with the tickets in his hand, 'but it's better that we leave on the first available boat.' So he did not think, even now, that they were completely safe, Netta deduced shrewdly, and kept her thoughts to herself when she surveyed the single-berth cabin that was to be her home for the voyage. Limited passenger accommodation exactly described it, she thought disparagingly, but she carefully refrained from saying so out loud. Instead,

'Where...?' she began, and stopped. She had asked him the same question in the cave, but the answer this time had to be very different. The bunk was narrow, functional, and definitely only meant to hold one. She was glad it was only meant to hold one, she told herself fiercely.

'Accommodation for ladies is to the fore of the vessel, the men's cabins are aft,' Joss read her thoughts with ease, and grinned at her rapidly rising colour.

'I only wanted to know,' she started sharply, and he interrupted her easily.

'Well, now you do. I shan't be very far away, don't worry.'

That was the least of her worries, she decided tartly, and was quickly to discover another, bigger one that occupied

85

the whole of her attention, even to the exclusion of the
gemstones round her waist. It was soon evident that the
cargo vessel did not ride like a liner, either. What cargo it
carried, she never discovered. Within less than an hour
after they got under way, she lost interest completely. It
could have been coconuts or car parts, for all she cared.
The first squall—Joss casually called them summer storms
—hit them shortly after they had eaten lunch. For a cargo
ship the food was very good, and Netta ate hungrily,
savouring familiar cooking once again, only to confess
ruefully soon afterwards,

'I wish I hadn't eaten that trifle for afters. I think it's
beginning to disagree with me.'

Joss showed no signs of discomfort, she thought resentfully, but aided by the wildly bucking motion of their
makeshift transport on the roughening sea, the disagree-
ment turned into a raging battle inside her, in which the
soup and the main course joined with unseemly enthusiasm. Netta fled for her cabin, and barely managed to
reach its blessed privacy before she and her recent lunch
parted company on the very worst of terms.

'Red hair and a green face go with one another quite
well,' Joss observed interestedly from the doorway of her
cabin.

'Go away,' she groaned.

'There's no place much I can go,' he answered con-
sideringly, and remained where he was. 'The deck's mostly
taken up with cargo.'

'Go anywhere. Overboard, if you like. But leave me
alone!' she wailed. She choked, gagged, and turned
desperately away from him, but instead of following her
uncharitable suggestion he stepped the rest of the way into
the cabin and held her head with expert hands until the
worst was over. Then he lifted her into the bunk and
sponged her face with blessedly cool water before he went
out. She heard the cabin door close softly behind him, and
hoped guiltily that he would be careful if he walked on
deck. She would never forgive herself if he did fall overboard. . . .

He came back again later. She did not know how much later, and she was too spent to care. She only wished he would go away and leave her alone. Overriding even the misery of seasickness was the fear paramount in her mind that Joss might discover the gemstones in her waistband. She felt him lift her up and lay her down again on fresh pillows, and whispered weakly,

'Leave me alone. I'll manage for myself.' Bitterly now she rued her promise to Ranjit, to deliver the jewels safely to his bank in London. Without them she could have sunk into merciful oblivion. Without them she might even have endured Joss's ministrations. Under other circumstances, her traitorous heart whispered, she might even have enjoyed them. She steeled herself to the feel of his arms about her as he lifted her up, despising herself for the longing that almost overwhelmed her, to turn her face into his shoulder, and let Ranjit and the jewels, indeed the rest of the world, pass her by.

It's the result of the weakness, it will pass, her weary mind insisted.

Give in, her equally weary heart begged, but she turned her face away, and stiffened her body against his hands, and somehow managed to stem the tears that longed to flow, because she was too proud to let Joss see them if they did. She refused to allow her heart to want a husband who had married her for expediency, and not for love. Who loved someone else. He had used her heart as a sacrifice to buy the safety of others, and then carelessly thrown that sacrifice away, unneeded, because the plane, after all, had gone without them.

'I'm thirsty.' Perhaps he would go away, if only to find someone to send with a drink. He went, but her relief was shortlived, because he returned with the drink himself.

'Sip this.' He held a glass of iced fruit juice to her lips, and she drank reluctantly. It was cold, and sweet, but it did little to revive her flagging energy. She fumbled at the neckband of her top, trying to ease the zip open in a bid to let in some cooler air, but her weakened fingers refused even this simple task, and her arms fell limply back on to the bunk.

'I'll do it for you.' Joss reduced the zip to instant obedience, and pulled the damp material loosely away from her burning skin. 'You'd be more comfortable if your waistband was loosened as well, it's far too tight in this heat,' he said critically, and reached down.

'No, leave it.' She tried to push his hands away, but they had not got sufficient strength for that, either. He put them aside with ease.

'Don't be silly,' he admonished her impatiently. 'I'm only loosening the zip, I'm not going to debag you.' He ignored her frantic, 'Please—don't....' and loosened the zip. Then he slid his fingers under the waistband, easing it away from her skin. 'You'll be cooler,' he began, then paused.

'He's found them!' Even before his fingers slid the rest of the way round her waistband, pausing at each hard bump on the way, she knew he had found them. He fingered the bumps under the cloth at first thoughtfully, and then with dawning comprehension and anger flicking across his face.

'You had the gemstones on you, all the time!' His eyes were as hard as the gold settings from which she had extracted the jewels. Hard, and accusing. 'You let me think you'd hidden them in the hotel,' he said harshly. 'You risked your life to bring them out. You should have told me.'

'And let you barter them to the rebels for my freedom?' she interrupted him shrilly. In spite of her weakness, she struggled upright on her pillows, and faced him with determined defiance. 'You assumed I'd left them in the hotel, I didn't tell you I'd done so. And I didn't tell you where they were, because it wasn't your concern,' she said firmly. 'The jewels are my responsibility, not yours.'

'They're my responsibility as well, now.' For a second a fleeting, unreadable expression displaced the anger deep in his eyes, but she was too occupied in shoring up her own crumbling defences to notice, and the next moment it had

gone, and the anger returned, and a determination stronger
than her own.

'The moment we dock you'll be free of any responsibility
towards me,' she retorted with spirit. 'You can have your
ring back the second we step ashore. For that matter, you
can have it back now.' Her hand moved to take it off.

'Keep it where it is.' His fingers closed over hers in a
grip that made her wince. She tried to pull her fingers
away. She could not bear his touch. It sabotaged her
determination, undermined her strength of mind. Her
heart raced with choking speed, but Joss held on to her
with ease, the force of his grip reflecting the inflexible
line of his jaw. 'Until those gems are deposited in a safe
place, you're not moving an inch from my side,' he gritted,
'and while you're with me, you'll wear my ring. I have a
right....'

'You took your rights in the cave!' she flung back at
him passionately, perilously close to tears. With a supreme
effort she controlled them, though she could not control the
shake in her voice. He had taken her, used her, when all
he wanted was Tara. She would never forgive him for
that. Any more than she would forgive herself for responding, for believing him, for being gullible enough to commit
herself before she gave a thought that there might be an
ulterior motive behind his lovemaking. She might yet have
to pay the penalty for her trust. She blanched at the
thought, and thrust it from her. She had enough problems
to contend with, she thought wearily, without adding another one that might never arise. Joss unexpectedly added
one himself.

'It's a good job I've already radioed the Home Office,
and warned them we're on our way.'

'What have the Home Office got to do with us?' She had
forgotten for the moment the nature of Joss's business in
Lak.

'They've warned the Customs people to expect us.'

'Customs?' She raised dismayed eyes to his, their clash
of wills temporarily forgotten. She had not given the
Customs check a thought.

'In case it hadn't occurred to you,' he could see it had not, she thought wrathfully, 'we'll be entering England without luggage, without papers, and without any means of identification. The Customs people will want answers to all sorts of questions.'

'Will the Home Office clear us?' If she was searched, who would believe she had a right to the gems? Fear rose in Netta, and she swallowed convulsively. With Lak in a state of siege, no one would be able to contact Ranjit. And even Joss, she suspected uneasily, might still not be entirely convinced of her right to the jewels.

'The Home Office will clear me,' he laid emphasis on the latter word, and her momentary relief died a swift death. 'I hope that as my wife you'll get the same free passage through.' He removed his hand from her fingers as he spoke, and his glance rested significantly on the ring. It winked back, deriding her helplessness, daring her to continue to defy him. 'Think about it,' Joss advised her coldly, and went out, leaving her mind in such a turmoil that she was scarcely capable of thinking about anything at all, except that as soon as she was free of the gems, she would also be free of her ring—and of Joss. Rebellion seemed to be in the fashion, she acknowledged drearily, because while her mind rejoiced at the prospect of all three, her heart told her mutinously it only wanted to be rid of the gems.

Later, she joined Joss at the rail, and watched the familiar white cliffs approaching with a trepidation they had never aroused in her before. Her legs felt curiously weak, and she told herself stoutly that it was the result of the rough passage they had had, but each time she thought of the coming Customs check she had qualms worse than anything the sea could produce. Even the rebels had not been able to rouse her to such a state of nerves, and when Joss told her curtly, 'When we reach the Customs, stay close to me, and leave me to do the talking,' for once she did as he bade her without protest.

'He won't need to kiss me to keep me quiet this time,' she told herself bitterly, and swallowed the lump that rose in her throat to mourn the omission. Her tongue clove to the roof of her mouth in parched paralysis, and she could not have spoken if she had wanted to when Joss sought out the first Customs and Excise uniform they encountered when they landed.

'Why does he have to attract attention?' she asked herself with frightened exasperation. 'Why can't we just file through, like any other passengers?' And all the time she knew they could not. Their bedraggled appearance, as well as their lack of papers and luggage, would attract attention of itself.

'We were warned you'd be coming, Mr de Courcey,' the uniformed man accompanying Joss bent a kindly eye on Netta's white face. If he did but realise it, his own presence had more to do with its lack of colour than her recent ordeals, but he went on, happily unaware, 'Your wife looks as if she's had a rough time, what with the sea voyage and all. You stay here, sir, and I'll go and see if your car's come.' He courteously handed Netta into a hard wooden chair, and bustled out, to return a few minutes later with the news, 'Your chauffeur's waiting for you, right outside the door. You'll soon be home,' he consoled with a smile, and Netta returned it weakly, her relief tempered by the unspoken question,

'Which home?'

'In London, as always,' her mind told her staunchly. 'At Thimbles, with Joss,' her heart implored.

'Ranjit's bank is in Chelsea,' she compromised with them both as she walked to the car with Joss.

'I'm afraid you're too late for the bank today, madam,' the chauffeur volunteered, 'and it's Bank Holiday weekend, too.'

'That means they'll be closed until Wednesday,' Joss observed.

'My father's safe is quite adequate,' Netta said shortly, which answered her heart, as well as her need for security for the gems, and wondered at the bleak depression that settled on her as she preceded Joss into the rear seat of the luxurious limousine, and heard him give her address to the chauffeur.

The housekeeper answered their knock, and her face reflected the same disconcerting dismay with which Wendy had greeted her arrival at the Embassy in Lak.

'I wasn't expecting you home for a while, Miss Netta.'

'What's going on?' Netta surveyed the bare hall, and the open door leading into what looked like an equally bare drawing room, with a puzzled frown.

'It's dry rot, miss,' came the gloomy answer.

'Dry rot? I thought we were having the house decorated?'

'We were. I mean, we are, when the boards have been seen to,' the housekeeper explained, 'but the men found the dry rot downstairs, and your father decided to have the house stripped and thoroughly checked over, and rewired at the same time. All the furniture's been sent into store except for the pieces in my room, and they'll be moving me out of that by the morning, I expect,' she predicted unhappily.

'That means the safe's gone, too?'

'The safe went to the bank, miss. Your father's going to be away for another few weeks, he's accepted an invitation to read his paper on diamonds to the Amsterdam Conference, after he's finished his business there, so he'll be away....'

'For another few weeks. You said.' Netta nodded in a preoccupied fashion. Her mind reeled. She could scarcely believe her evil luck. After coming all this way, now they had at last reached England she still could not rid herself of the burdensome gems. 'My clothes?' More than anything else, she needed a change of clothes. Surely not all of those had gone, as well?

'Your clothes all went along with your furniture, into store, miss. You won't be able to get at them until your father comes home and gives instructions for the furniture to come back. We didn't expect you yet, you see,' the housekeeper reiterated maddeningly.

Netta stared at her, stunned. Even in England, she was still a refugee. She not only had nowhere to put the gems, but she herself had neither a change of clothing, nor a roof under which she could find reasonable shelter.

'I'll find a hotel somewhere close by.' She paused, struck by another thought. She could not go into a hotel in her present dilapidated state, and without luggage. And if she had clothes, she would not dare to change them and leave her slacks and their priceless waistband in a hotel wardrobe.

'I don't know what to suggest, I'm sure,' the housekeeper began worriedly. 'It's a problem, with no furniture in the house.'

'It's no problem,' Joss assured her crisply, 'my wife will be coming home with me.'

'Your—wife?'

Netta could have slapped him. The housekeeper's shocked eyes flew to her left hand, and Netta resisted an urge to thrust it into her slacks pocket, out of sight.

'We were married in Lak. It's a long story,' she intervened hastily.

'It sounds remarkably short notice to me,' the older woman said disapprovingly. 'Does your father know, Miss Netta?' she asked, in a voice that Netta recognised from when she was very small, and wont to bring home stray puppies at inconvenient moments. An hysterical giggle rose inside her at the thought of likening Joss to a stray puppy, and she stifled it hastily. Now was not the time for hilarity.

'Mr Vaughan will be told when he returns from abroad,' Joss said smoothly, in a tone that made it plain he had no intention of giving explanations to a housekeeper, however valued a member of the household she might be. 'In the meantime, I think food is indicated.' He gave the older woman a polite nod, took Netta by the arm, and steered her firmly towards the car.

'Where shall I contact you, if your father rings, Miss Netta?' the housekeeper called after them.

'Thimbles, at Long Minton,' Joss said firmly.

'I'll let you know when I find a hotel,' Netta called back.

Twin daggers of determination and defiance flashed between them as their eyes met, and Netta ducked hastily into the car as the chauffeur held open the back door. Lunch would give her a reprieve, she thought thankfully. With a sense of surprise she realised she felt hungry. Food in a relaxed atmosphere might give her the inspiration she needed to circumvent Joss, and solve her difficulty at the same time.

She eased herself into the far corner of the back seat, deliberately putting as much distance between them as possible. A tab protruded from the top of the hide cushion, and she pulled it experimentally. As she expected, it brought down a central armrest, and she slid it out to its full extent across the seat between them. It was just the barrier she needed, she thought with satisfaction. She felt Joss's glance slide coldly across at her, but she refused to meet it. She was in England now, and their 'honeymoon', if such it could be called, she thought bitterly, was over, as were the humiliations and the trials of her dependence upon him. Now she was home she could return to her old, free independence. She owed no allegiance to Joss, rather it was the other way around; he had blackmailed her into marrying him. She used the phrase deliberately, keeping her anger alive. And now it was over. She ignored the pang that shot through her at the thought, although she could not ignore the inescapable fact that the unawakened, heart-whole girl who had journeyed outward so lightheartedly would never again inhabit the empty, aching shell of her former self, which was all she had returned to England with.

'Where had you in mind to eat, sir?' The chauffeur spoke as if they were dressed in their best clothes, and out for a social occasion, and Netta's desire to giggle returned. Suddenly, everything seemed unreal. The rebels, the burning brush, the gunshots and the plane roaring out of reach over their heads. The cave—she did not want to think about the cave—and the river and the rough sea. And now, in complete contrast, the sleek car bowling smoothly between quiet fields, which stretched out in front of the long bonnet in a seemingly endless procession, the streets of London already left behind.

'We'll throw ourselves on Mrs Berry's mercy, I think,' Joss answered, and the chauffeur's peaked cap nodded.

'She'll be prepared for you, sir. I phoned her when we set off, just in case.'

Joss seemed to attract the same sort of instant service at home that he had done abroad, and Netta hoped uneasily that it was not a big restaurant they were going to. In her present state of dress she did not feel like inviting stares from the other diners. But the 'Mrs Berry' sounded reassuring. It was probably some small country pub which Joss frequented, and where he was well enough known to gain special attention, she consoled herself.

Perhaps she could get a room there for herself, over the period of the holiday weekend? The possibility sharpened her attention, and she sat up. It would solve her problem beautifully. Then she could return to London and deposit the gems in Ranjit's bank, get herself some decent clothes, and go to a hotel in town until her father returned home. Of course! That would provide the ideal solution. Her flagging spirits revived miraculously at the ease with which her problems could be settled.

'If only I'd given myself time to think, I needn't have got into such a state about it in the first place,' she berated herself scornfully. The nervous strain of the last weeks had affected her more than she realised, dulling her usual clarity of mind. It seemed like a good omen that her powers of thought were already reasserting themselves.

The problem of her marriage would no doubt be solved just as easily, she told herself with new-found optimism. All that she needed to do, once she was rid of the gems, was to return Joss's ring, go back to London, and instigate proceedings for an annulment. She need not wait for Joss to take the initiative. If she started the proceedings herself, it would show him she did not care. She could unburden herself, and leave the whole disastrous episode behind her.

As well as her heart?

She blinked at the sudden stinging sensation at the back of her eyes, and turned hastily to look out of the car window.

'It's probably a cold coming,' she sought feebly for an excuse for her optic discomfort. 'It's probably the change in climate.'

But the fields outside the car windows lay basking in warm summer sunshine, and even in her light safari suit she felt not the slightest chill. Only a cold, gripping pain in the region of her heart that seemed to have become a constant companion from the time she promised, reluctantly, 'I will.'

The fields went on, and on. At last she turned to Joss and forced herself to speak.

'We've come a long way out of town, just to get a meal. How far away is this Mrs Berry of yours?'

She sensed the answer even before it came. It spoke to her from his easy assurance, from the cool authority in the glance that he turned on her, and it ignited an explosive anger inside her that took away the hunger, and the tiredness, and even the ache about her heart.

'Mrs Berry is the housekeeper at Thimbles,' he said coolly. 'We're going home for an early dinner.'

'Your home. . . .'

She choked on the words, fury depriving her momentarily of the power of speech. She swallowed hard, and tried again, but remembered, just in time, the chauffeur sitting quietly, but alert, in front of them. Pride forbade her to argue in front of a servant. As Joss knew it would, she realised, even further incensed. He had timed it with beautiful accuracy so that she would not realise where she was going until it was too late to do anything about it. Virtually kidnapping her.

'How dare you!'

She bit her lip savagely to stem the tirade of condemnation that boiled up inside her—would have boiled over, but for the presence of the chauffeur.

'Thimbles is more comfortable than a hotel,' he said calmly, 'you'll be better looked after there.' He meant the gems would be better looked after, she thought furiously, and blanched as a fresh, more personal implication of their destination dawned upon her seething mind.

She had not got a stitch of clothing with her except for the battered, mud-stained, disreputable outfit that she stood up in. And she was on her way to Thimbles, as Joss's wife, to meet Joss's family.

And Tara....

CHAPTER NINE

'THERE'S Thimbles.'

Joss's voice reached Netta across a wall of silence. She retreated behind it like a protective barrier, vibrant with suppressed emotion. She resented him breaking through. It was a liberty, an intrusion of her privacy.

'Over there, through that gap in the trees.'

Joss stepped across the barrier as if it was not there, and the anger inside her erupted, tearing aside the flimsy remnants of her self-control. She stiffened, then rounded on him, and opened her mouth to let the angry words pour out.

'I'll stop the car for you for a minute or two, madam. The view of the house from here is particularly fine.' The chauffeur spoke first, unaware of the impending storm his words had interrupted. His hand moved, and he pressed a button on the console which slid the car window down on Netta's side until it disappeared into the door aperture, leaving her with an uninterrupted view.

She did not want to look at the view. She would much rather have done without the chauffeur's consideration and gone straight on to Thimbles, and got the ordeal over as quickly as possible. Her nerves crackled with tension at the mere thought of meeting Joss's people. She did not even know if they lived at Thimbles. He had never spoken to her of his family. Only of Tara. . . .

'It smells good.' Joss took a deep, satisfied breath as a warm breeze wafted through the window, bringing with it the scents of high summer to mingle with the leather smell of the car upholstery. He leaned across to look out of the window with her. The armrest got in his way, and he flicked it upwards, back into the slot from whence it had come, so that there was no longer any physical barrier between them. He slid along the seat into the space that the

98

armrest had occupied, and Netta felt him press against her shoulder, not hard, just touching, too intent on catching the first glimpse of his home to notice that he was crowding her. To notice that she was there at all.

She moved uneasily, wishing there was more space between her and the side of the car, to allow her to move away from him. Wishing he had left the armrest where it was, that the house stood on his side of the car. The touch of his shoulder against her own set her pulses racing with a clamorous awareness of him that she thought she had conquered when they left the cave. Now it broke through her frail defences with a terrifying ease that warned her she had not left the battle behind her when she left Lak.

'You can see the house more clearly in the winter, when the trees are bare.'

They framed it now. Unwillingly, her eyes followed his pointing finger, across the low hedge that flanked the climbing lane in a wild tangle of honeysuckle and foxgloves. She caught her breath. Why did the foxglove spots have to remind her so sharply of the exotic velvet blobs which broke the bright gold of the tua lilies in the drawing room at the Embassy, during the mockery that was her wedding ceremony?

The high-standing corn beyond the hedge wavered suddenly across her vision, and she blinked hard, willing the curve of the river below it to remain still. The waters danced crystal clear in the sunlight—no sluggish poisoned river this—and led her eyes upwards again from the opposite bank across green parkland to the gap in the trees that formed the end of a graceful ride.

'They were planted when my great-grandfather was born.' Joss spoke matter-of-factly, accepting the caring that planted for generations still to come. A caring that even through her anger Netta sensed he would carry on. The hand that planted the parallel rows of widely spaced, venerable park giants had done so with an eye to pleasing the senses, as well as providing shade, she saw. No unimaginative rank of swiftly maturing poplars, these. Limes abounded, she could smell their perfume mingling with the scent of honeysuckle from the hedge, and hear the low-toned hum of their attendant bees even from this distance. There were chestnuts, too, that must look glorious in their spring blossom, but now bore a prickly weight of swelling fruit. Conkers, such as children love to gather. Joss's children. His—and Tara's? Her anger sharpened, shoring up her defences, so that her voice sounded almost normal when she spoke.

'It's Tudor period.' No one, however angry, could re-main indifferent to such gracious loveliness, and her eyes feasted on the low lines of the manor house that was her destination. The dark timber framing dissected the her-ringbone pattern of red brick-like veins in an old hand, warmly coloured in the sunshine, and serene in its sylvan setting. Joss must have sensed her reluctant interest, be-cause he volunteered,

'The first Jocelyn de Courcey started it, when he came back from the wars. His son carried on the building, and since then, like Topsy, it's "just growed".' Joss smiled, but the smile was for his home, and not for her, and Netta thrust down an unwelcome pang. At least she had been right about the period, she thought with satisfaction. She remembered Wendy saying that Joss's family went back to Agincourt.

'Its "growed", as you call it, very nicely,' she commented drily as the car swung on to a wide gravel sweep, and drew to a halt in front of the house, and she was able to inspect it at close quarters. Age had matured the various periods of building into one harmonious whole, helped by the sensi-tive care with which the original concept had been en-larged and extended by subsequent owners, using similar materials and pattern of architecture. 'It's beautiful,' she breathed, unable to hide her admiration.

'I didn't know you were interested in architecture.' Joss half turned towards her, then broke off as a wild barking sounded from somewhere inside what looked like a stable block standing away to the side of the house. A weather vane glinted in the sun from the centre of the roof, point-ing the breeze from the south.

There were a lot of things Joss did not know about her, Netta thought dispiritedly. There was one vital thing he must never learn, and that was the secret longing locked deep in her heart, to which she only had the key. 'And I've thrown that away, for good,' she told herself with conviction. She felt in control of herself again, now that she was free from the confinement of the car, free from immediate contact with Joss. He stood a foot or two away from her on the gravel, his head raised, listening.

'I wonder if she remembers?' he murmured, almost to himself.

'Dogs don't forget, sir, even if they're young,' the chauffeur spoke with assurance. 'Will Dyer carried on training her for you when you went abroad, and normally a word from him will quieten her.' The man smiled tolerantly. 'From the noise she's making now, she must have heard your voice, and recognised it.'

'Let's try her.' Joss whistled once, and waited. The barking stopped, then started again on an almost hysterical note, until someone's hand appeared over the stable door and pushed it open. Without waiting for it to swing fully ajar, a slim russet body hurtled through the opening and made towards Joss at top speed. There was no question that the dog remembered. Joss went down on one knee with a low delighted laugh that had in it a sudden catch. He held out his arms, and the young Irish setter dived headlong into them, with threshing tail and licking tongue, and gruff little whimpers that left no doubt who it acknowledged as its master. Netta felt a sudden lump rise in her throat, and swallowed hard. This was a side of Joss she had not seen before, a warm, affectionate side, so different from the tough, self-sufficient shell which was all he had ever presented towards herself, and against which she had hammered in vain, only to fall back bruised and defeated. A swift stab of pure jealousy speared through her as she watched him wind his arms about the dog, fondling it with unashamed affection. He had held her in his arms too, but his affection then had been feigned, aimed only at silencing her. And she had basked in the warmth of its illusion, until the sun went in and left her shrinking from the bitter wind of reality. For her, there was no joyous homecoming.

'Let's see how well she's taken Will's training.' Joss caught at Netta's hand and drew her away from the dog towards the house. His touch was indifferent, impersonal, his attention solely on the red setter. 'Stay!' he commanded, and Netta raised her head, startled. Where had she heard him say that before?

Joss drew her with him across the gravel, but she only half saw where she was going, her mind was busily seeking backwards, teased by the elusive memory, and then the dog whined sharply, bringing her back to her surroundings. Joss paused, and looked back over his shoulder, to where the young setter stood beside the car, quivering, begging him to let her come to him.

'Stay, Tara. Stay!' he ordered firmly.

'Tara? Did you call her—Tara?' Netta spun round, and snatched her hand away from his. She knew, now, where she had heard the order before. For a second or two, a mist seemed to dance in front of her eyes.

'That's her name,' Joss laughed down at her, enjoying his bombshell. 'Who did you think Tara was?' he asked her. 'If you remember, I told you her hair was the same colour as yours.' He said her hair was flat. The setter had a flat coat. She understood, now, the amusement she had seen in his eyes when he told her. A tight band of fury seemed to constrict her chest, making it difficult for her to breathe. Once again Joss had deliberately deceived her, cruelly inflicted on her a night of misery and uncertainty and torment that returned in a wave to wash over her.

'How could you?' she gasped in a strangled whisper. 'How could. . . .'

'Joss! How marvellous, darling!'

First the chauffeur saved him from her anger, then the girl. A member of his family? A sister, perhaps? She ran from the front door of the house, not with quite the same speed as the red setter, but with the same singleness of purpose. She ignored Netta and the chauffeur as if they

were not there, and made straight for Joss, though Netta
had an uncanny feeling that the pale blue eyes missed no
detail of her own person, nor her clothes, which immediately felt ten times more bedraggled than before in contrast with the undeniable chic of the other girl's appearance. She exuded expensive grooming, from her pale green
linen dress and dainty high-heeled matching sandals to the
tip of her flaxen hair, which was done up in a French
pleat, with not a wisp out of place.

'Masses of lacquer,' Netta judged ill-humouredly, and
fought down a flood of possessive fury which rose inside
her as the newcomer flung both her arms round Joss's
neck and swung her feet from off the floor. She had to return them to terra firma fairly rapidly, Netta saw with
malicious satisfaction, since Joss did not wrap his arms
round her and hold her up, as she obviously hoped he
would. It would have taken quite a bit of doing anyway,
Netta decided uncharitably, since the fair-haired girl was
almost as tall as Joss, although she was slim to the point of
being angular. Joss's response seemed somewhat tardy,
and she thought he looked decidedly surprised at the
newcomer's appearance, though he kissed her warmly
enough to send another stab through Netta, and she stirred
restlessly. She did not want Joss herself, so why should
she bother who he kissed? she asked herself defiantly, but
she could not shrug off the blanketing weight of depression
that settled on her as her head and her heart gave her two
different answers at once.

'It's marvellous to be back,' Joss agreed enthusiastically,
and turned to Netta. 'Come and say hello to my cousin
Caroline,' he bade her.

So she was his cousin, not his sister. And although she
told herself she had no right to feel possessive about Joss,
she could not help the grudging reluctance with which she
joined the pair.

'Oh—hello.' The fair-haired girl swivelled a look in
Netta's direction as if she noticed her for the first time, and
Netta's lips tightened. The family all seemed to be tarred
with the same brush, she thought censoriously. Joss had

not offered to shake hands with her when they were first
introduced, and neither did Caroline, and his first greeting
to her had had about it the same lack of cordiality as his
cousin's. She gave the other girl a cool nod, and resolutely
kept her own small fist firmly in her jacket pocket.

'Come on in home, do,' Caroline returned Netta's greeting in kind, and turned back to Joss immediately, still
clinging closely to his arm.

So Caroline called Thimbles 'home', Netta noted, and
wondered if the word had been used deliberately for her
benefit, to make her feel an outsider. She needn't have
bothered, she thought abrasively. I couldn't feel more of an
outsider in this family, if I tried. Not that it mattered. As
soon as her father returned home, she would be able to
leave Thimbles, and Joss. Leave them to Caroline? An
upsurge of revulsion at the prospect caught her by surprise,
and impulsively she stepped out so as not to be left behind as the two set off towards the house, leaving her to
follow or not as she wished.

'Come!' She snapped her fingers to the red setter. At
least the dog wagged its tail to her, she thought, and felt
unaccountably comforted when it answered her summons,
and stopped long enough for her to caress its soft ears as it
passed.

'Tara seems to have taken to you, madam,' the chauffeur
smiled. 'I've never known her to take notice of anyone before, except Will Dyer and the master.'

'She doesn't want to let him out of her sight, that's all.'
Caroline's look challenged Netta's right to give an order
to Joss's dog. 'Down, Tara! She's over-excited.' She flap-
ped a beautifully manicured hand at the setter, which con-
sidering she had just said it was over-excited was not the
most sensible thing to do. The young animal took it to be
a signal for play, and with a joyful bark it jumped up
against Caroline with both front paws on her dress. 'Get
down!' Caroline staggered back against Joss as if the dog
had been a fully grown St Bernard pushing against her,
instead of a lightweight setter, and Netta's lips curled.
Joss's cousin was missing no opportunity to demonstrate

that she belonged at Thimbles. And Joss belonged to her?

'Down, Tara!' Joss quietened the dog sternly.

'Look at my dress,' his cousin wailed, 'it's marked all down the front! I'll have to go in and change.'

'It'll brush off, it's only dry dust.' The gravel was bone dry, and the slight mark would shake off the linen with ease, Netta judged.

'You should have left the dog where it was until I called her.' Joss turned on Netta with a frown of displeasure.

'Eh, Mr Joss, but it's good to have you home again!' A buxom, beaming figure appeared in the house doorway, and Joss's face lit up with pleasure, chasing the frown away.

'Mrs Berry!' At least she knew who Mrs Berry was, Netta thought, and realised suddenly that she felt desperately hungry.

Joss kissed the white-haired woman soundly on both cheeks, in a manner that made Netta suspect—correctly, she afterwards discovered—that the housekeeper had at one time been his nurse, and she forgot some of her ire at his manner towards herself as she watched him. Back home, among his own people, he appeared in an entirely different light, a warmer, more human one, than the 'Renard' she knew.

'I'm starving!' he echoed her own thoughts, and the housekeeper's smile grew even broader, if that were possible.

'I've got your favourite for you,' she announced in a pleased voice, 'it'll be ready just as soon as you are. A nice mixed grill, some fresh picked mushrooms ... I'll go and see how the cooking's getting on, while Johnson brings your luggage up to your room.'

'We haven't got any luggage for him to bring up,' Joss said ruefully. 'We got away from Lak with our lives, and just what we stood up in, and lucky to do that. I wonder, Caroline,' he turned to his cousin, 'could you fit Netta out with some clothes until she can get to the shops after the Bank Holiday?' Manlike, it did not occur to him that there might be any difficulty in that direction.

'I'll make do until I can get something for myself,'

Netta refused promptly. She would rather wear rags than put on anything belonging to Caroline, she thought mutinously. Even if it would fit, which it wouldn't, since the other girl was very much taller, and a good deal broader in build.

'We're the wrong size for one another.' Caroline somehow managed to sound regretful, Netta thought cynically, and it flashed across her mind that the other girl would make a formidable opponent. And then she wondered why she should regard Caroline as an opponent, when she had nothing she wanted to contest possession of. Certainly not Joss, she told herself stoutly.

'Your little friend is rather small,' Caroline went on smoothly, and Netta's lips tightened. The girl made her sound as if she was stunted, she thought angrily, but before she could think of a suitable retort, Mrs Berry intervened.

'Miss Rosemary's clothes would be a better fit than Miss Healey-Smythe's,' she suggested comfortably. 'They're about the same dainty build.' So much for Caroline's spite, Netta thought with a grateful glance at the housekeeper. 'I'll instruct Mary what to get for you, and we'll soon fit you out in something pretty,' she went on in a friendly voice, and Netta warmed to the first real welcome she had received at Thimbles, except from Tara. 'I'm sure Miss Rosemary wouldn't mind. If you'd like to come along with me, Miss—er——' she invited.

'What a good idea,' Caroline enthused, 'and while you're away, Joss and I can have a nice long talk. Take your time, Miss—er——' she ran into the same difficulty as the housekeeper.

'I'm not "Miss" anything,' Netta stated flatly. Since Joss did not offer to introduce her, she thought furiously, it was high time she made herself known. Maybe she should have waited for him to speak. He opened his mouth as if he was about to, but she rushed on regardless, silencing him effectively. Maybe it was the backlash of anger because of the way he had deceived her over Tara; over many other things, which she preferred not to think about now. Perhaps Caroline's manner goaded her into it. But whatever it was that drove her, she had no cause for complaint about the effect of her announcement on the others.

'I'm Mrs de Courcey,' she introduced herself bluntly. 'Joss's wife,' she underlined her status in a clear voice.

'Joss's—*what*?'

It was the reverse of congratulatory—and slightly overdone. Caroline's artistically painted eyebrows rose in a haughty arc, but Netta sensed her surprise was not as genuine as she would have liked her audience to believe. She turned to Joss with a deeply wounded expression.

'You didn't tell me you were thinking of getting married, Joss darling. You didn't let me know.'

As an exhibition of hurt feelings, it was well done, except for the faintly calculating gleam in the other girl's pale blue eyes that Netta detected easily enough, but thought wryly that Joss, being a man, probably would not.

'We didn't know ourselves until half an hour before the ceremony,' she stated evenly, without giving him a second in which to explain. She did not see any reason why she should hide his conduct, she thought mutinously, nor her own false position as his wife. Making it plain to other people helped to bolster up her own determination to remedy that position at the earliest opportunity, and she could see no logical reason for the sudden sick feeling that assailed her, of having burned her boats behind her. 'After we were married,' she carried on deliberately in a firm voice, 'we were too busy keeping one step ahead of the rebels who were hunting for us to have time to post announcements.'

Let them make what they pleased of her announcement now! she thought uncaringly, and kept her chin high, facing Caroline's hostility with fierce pride. She had her back to Joss, so she did not see the quick gleam that came into his eyes, that might or might not have been anger towards her for taking the situation into her own hands, without giving him the opportunity to make his own explanation. He had done the same thing with her father's housekeeper, Netta thought with satisfaction, so this was simply tit for tat.

'I expect Mr Joss will tell you all about it, while I take

Mrs de Courcey upstairs and find her a change of clothes.'
Mrs Berry's voice cut across the sudden crackling silence
that dropped between them, and Netta looked across at her
suspiciously. Was there just a hint of laughter in the warm,
kindly voice, as she spoke to Caroline? 'Perhaps you'd like
to come with me now, madam?' She offered Netta an
avenue of escape. 'You'll be able to put all those awful
things behind you, now you're home, and you can relax
and be comfortable,' the housekeeper went on hospitably.

'I shan't be staying for long,' Netta announced in a
clipped voice. 'Only during the Bank Holiday weekend,
then I'll be returning to London.' She had already made her
position as Joss's wife abundantly clear, she decided hardly,
so she might as well make her future intentions even
clearer, to Joss, as well as to Mrs Berry and Caroline.

With her head held high she followed the motherly
figure through the doorway. She did not look at either
Joss or Caroline as she passed them. She did not dare to
look at Joss, although she was warmly conscious that the
red setter padded behind her across the tiled floor of the
hall, accompanying her to the foot of the wide, curving
staircase that wound upwards to a balcony landing above
and disappeared into what seemed to be a wing of the
house away to the left.

'Stay!' she told Tara, automatically forbidding the dog
access to the upstairs rooms, and immediately winced as
she heard her own voice repeat Joss's order. She wished
she could feel some satisfaction that Tara obeyed her, she
thought forlornly, the setter sat obediently at the foot of
the stairs, and watched her with liquid eyes as she
mounted, but instead of jubilation all she felt was a weariness of spirit descend on her like a grey blanket, so that
her usual fleetness of foot deserted her, and she had to
reach for the banister rail to help pull herself upwards.
Luckily, Mrs Berry's ample girth made her slow in ascend-
ing, so it did not look unnatural that Netta paused as well
when they reached the landing and looked over the carved
rails into the hall below—and gasped as Joss's eyes
speared her to the spot across the cool, shadowed distance.

'Let's go into the drawing room, darling, we can talk in comfort there.'

Vaguely she heard Caroline speak, felt irritation rise in her at the girl's persistent use of the word 'darling' which, coming from Caroline, had in it a showbiz kind of emptiness that repelled her. She watched the pale green dress disappear through a doorway leading off the hall, and saw Joss start to follow her. He was half way across the hall in his cousin's wake, and Netta thought herself safe from observation, when he suddenly paused, as if he sensed she was watching him. He stopped and raised his head, and looked up straight at her.

She caught her breath and a thrill of something like fear ran through her veins. Her legs longed to run, to flee to some sanctuary where she need not meet the compelling glow in those strange, golden eyes. But she could not move. His look rooted her to the spot. Her legs would not run, and her eyes could not look away. And the expression in his narrowed glance told her that, far from returning to London as soon as the Bank Holiday weekend was over, she would leave Thimbles only when he—Joss—decided he would let her go.

CHAPTER TEN

IT seemed a hundred years before he turned away.

When at last he dropped his eyes, and followed his cousin into the drawing room, and the heavy door shut behind him cutting him off, Netta held on to the banister and shook all over. The palms of her hands felt wet, and for a dreadful minute she thought she was going to faint. She clung on to the carved wood as if it were a lifeline, while the landing, and the hall below, spun in a crazy dance in front of her blurred vision.

'The rooms in the master suite are lovely and bright. They face the morning sun.'

Mrs Berry's voice steadied her, and she turned as the housekeeper opened a door further along the landing and beckoned Netta to follow her inside.

Sanctuary! The bedroom welcomed her like a light at the end of a dark tunnel, and she stumbled towards it, relief keeping her on her feet. To have privacy—a room of her own.... She was through the door before the sense of what the housekeeper said penetrated her mind.

The master suite?

She had expected to be placed in a small guest bedroom, and her knees nearly failed her altogether when she viewed the accommodation which she was being offered. The room was huge, and as the housekeeper said, it was light, with long, leaded windows on two walls. Her feet sank into a soft embossed carpet, and at any other time she would have delighted in the beauty of the furnishings, which blended in a perfectly chosen admixture of antique and modern to offer aesthetic pleasure and luxurious comfort to the fortunate occupant.

'Your bathroom's through this door, madam,' Mrs Berry drew her into the room with obvious pride, 'and Mr Joss's bathroom leads off his dressing room, through here.'

Netta hardly heard her. The bed drew her eyes like a magnet. It was large, like the room, an amply proportioned double-sized fourposter—and it was made up for two. There would be no need for her to ask this time where Joss would sleep. It was perfectly obvious where Mrs Berry thought they were both going to sleep.

'No!'

'I beg your pardon, madam?'

'Oh—er—nothing.' Netta gathered her scattered wits with difficulty. Mrs Berry was not to know. Until the chauffeur telephoned her, she could not know that they were even on their way. But in that case, how had the chauffeur found out? He had been there at the docks to meet them. Perhaps the Home Office had. . . .

'It's good to have the master suite in use again,' Mrs Berry beamed at her happily. 'The old Earl never used it —being a bachelor, he didn't bother. He used to keep it ready for Mr Joss's parents to use when they came, but that didn't last long, poor souls.' She shook her head sadly, then brightened. 'It's time Thimbles had a bride again.' Her eyes were soft as she turned them on Netta. 'Eh, but it was wonderful news when we had Mr Joss's cable from the ship, to tell us he was on his way home at last, and bringing his wife with him, and would we open up the master suite for you both.'

'Joss cabled you?' Netta's voice was a choked whisper. He had not said a word to herself about what he had done. She shrugged aside the fact that for the greater part of the voyage she had been prostrate with seasickness. The moment she was on her feet again Joss should have told her. No, asked her. As it was, he acted on the high-handed assumption that she would fall in with whatever plans he had in mind, whether she was willing or otherwise, and she writhed impotently under the ease with which he had succeeded. So far! she told herself angrily, and turned her back on the bed.

'Well now, didn't he tell you?' the housekeeper asked her in a surprised voice. 'It's not like Mr Joss to be secretive. But perhaps he wanted to surprise you.'

The Joss she knew would probably surprise Mrs Berry, thought Netta acidly, but she did not say so out loud. There was no point in causing any more dissent in the house, particularly as she did not intend to remain there for more than a few days, however attractive her surroundings. It was sufficient to ward off Caroline's hostility, without incurring Mrs Berry's displeasure as well. Joss was obviously the apple of her eye.

'It's a good thing you were a week or two on the way. It gave us more time to prepare for you.'

'We were on a cargo ship,' Netta replied absently. Talking helped to restore her poise, and she carried on in a firmer voice, 'The vessel called in at most of the major ports on the way back, loading and unloading cargo, which was why the journey took so long.' It had taken weeks, and seemed like years. 'The room is quite beautiful,' she added, with an obvious sincerity that brightened the housekeeper's smile. At least she could be truthful about that, she thought thankfully as the elderly woman told her helpfully,

'Mary's bringing you some clothes, and you'll find all you need in the bathroom. Miss Rosemary always keeps it stocked for when she comes to stay here.'

'Miss Rosemary?' Joss should have at least sketched in an outline of his family for her, since he had virtually brought her to his home by force, and she blamed him resentfully for her lack of knowledge, which must make the housekeeper wonder. She smarted under the necessity of gaining information about his people in such a manner, though Mrs Berry did not seem to think it was at all untoward, and went on placidly,

'Miss Rosemary is Mr Joss's sister. She's married, and living abroad now, but she comes home every year to visit. The old Earl brought them both up, after their parents were killed in a car smash when they were very young. They were like his own, to him. And since he never married, they were the only family he had who were really close to him.'

Which probably explained why Joss had inherited Thimbles, and not the title. Netta had only the vaguest of notions about the rules governing such matters, but she knew a profound thankfulness that she was free from the entanglements such a position would have brought in its train. As plain Mrs de Courcey she could take steps to have their marriage annulled without attracting unwelcome publicity.

'That sounds like Mary now. Come on in and show Mrs de Courcey what you've brought for her,' Mrs Berry instructed the fresh-faced country girl of about nineteen, who appeared through the door with her arms full of clothes, and regarded Netta with a friendly smile and frank interest.

'Look after Mrs de Courcey while I go and supervise the cooking,' the housekeeper bade her, and turned to Netta. 'I'll call you in about three quarters of an hour,' she promised, and bustled away.

'You must be feeling hungry by now,' Mary said sympathetically. 'But Mrs Berry's cooking's worth waiting for,' she added with disarming frankness, and Netta smiled.

'I'm starving,' she confessed, 'but I need a bath even more than I need food.' The ablutionary provisions on board the cargo vessel had been adequate but spartan, and her longing for perfumed soap had not diminished since her night in the cave.

'I'll go and run your bath for you, while you get undressed,' Mary offered obligingly. 'There's a robe here,' she laid it carefully across the bed, and put a selection of dresses beside it for choice, and a pile of dainty underwear. The robe and one of the dresses were in a pale, creamy primrose, the former daisy-sprigged, and the latter plain.

'They're lovely,' Netta smiled her thanks. 'Primrose is one of my favourite colours.'

'Mrs Berry said as how you'd got red hair, miss—I mean ma'am—and the two don't shout at one another, do they? You has to be careful, with red hair.'

'They go beautifully together,' Netta laughed out loud, the tensions of the past hours finding an unexpected safety valve in amusement at Mary's unorthodox view of fashion. 'Your gardener must think along the same lines,' she

remembered. 'I noticed a lovely clump of yellow hollyhocks set against a corner of the house, as we rounded the
drive.' The red herringbone-patterned brick made a perfect foil for the tall, old-fashioned loveliness of the papery
powderpuff flowers, which were just at their peak of
blooming, and gave the ancient house a warm, homely
touch as if to welcome anyone approaching.

'Yes, but hollyhocks aren't just for colour, are they?'
Mary said practically.

'Surely you don't use them for culinary purposes? For
cooking?' Netta elucidated, as Mary turned on her a look
of puzzled incomprehension. She had heard of a lot of
peculiar plants being used in such a way, but never hollyhocks before.

'Lor' no, you'd be poisoned for sure,' Mary laughed
merrily. 'But you've got to have a clump of hollyhocks,
haven't you? They say as it keeps love in the house, does
a clump of hollyhocks,' she imparted her simple wisdom as
she opened the bathroom door, and Netta heard her hum-
ming happily to herself over the sound of running water.

'It keeps love in the house. . . .'

Maybe it did, but not for herself and Joss. For Caroline
and Joss, perhaps. For Caroline and Joss, certainly, if
Caroline had her way. Netta sat down on the edge of the
bed rather suddenly. The couch she had just vowed to
herself she would not go near, but her knees refused to
hold her, and she had no choice. Her fingers trembled so
that they fumbled on the buttons of her shirtwaister top,
and it was only the increased volume of Mary's rendering
of '. . . 'tis love, and love alone, my heart is seeking,' sung
with more enthusiasm than regard for tune, that made her
realise the taps had stopped running. Hurriedly she dis-
robed, and slipped on the pretty cotton robe, and mentally
blessed her unknown sister-in-law's taste for clothing
which, like her size, exactly accorded with Netta's own.
Without having met Rosemary, she knew they would like
one another. Which was not of much use—sharp pain
pierced her at the thought—since they would never have
the opportunity to get to know one another.

'I've run the water nice and deep for you.' It was plain that Mary liked her bath that way, and could think of no greater favour to bestow on someone—Netta realised with a sense of shock—someone whom the young maid must regard as the new mistress of Thimbles. She considered her position. For some reason, it was something she had not thought about before—and must not think of now. Mary would learn the true situation soon enough, she thought grimly, and found herself envying the young maid's uncomplicated outlook on life, and hoping that no one would ever spoil her simple trust. It would be like trampling on a daisy. She herself had trusted Joss....

'I'll take your clothes downstairs with me when I go, and give them a good wash for you,' her young helper offered generously, and jolted Netta back to a sense of reality like an electric shock. Mary must not be allowed to touch her safari suit. No one must be allowed to touch that. Being at Thimbles had given her a false sense of security, but it did not alter the priceless value of the gemstones in her waistband. Mary eyed her slacks critically. 'My, but they've had a bad time!' She regarded the stains left by the river mud, and which would probably never come out of the material now. 'I'll try and get it clean for you, otherwise the only way would be to dye the whole suit,' and reached for it across the bed.

'Never mind the suit,' Netta grabbed it from her hastily. 'I washed it on the boat coming over, so it's clean, though as you say the stains probably won't ever come out now.' She became aware that the homely little face opposite was regarding her with hurt surprise. 'It's no reflection on your capabilities,' she hastened to assure Mary, 'but the suit itself isn't worth a lot of work.' It was worth a fortune, and the possibility of even one of the smallest of Ranjit's diamonds disappearing down a washing machine waste pipe filled her with horror. 'It's just that—just that——' she searched desperately for an explanation that would satisfy the young girl, and salve her pride at the same time. 'It's just that I want to keep my suit as a souvenir,' she finished lamely, and went weak with relief as Mary's face brightened.

'Of course you do, how silly of me. Anyone would want to keep the clothes they were married in.'

How mistaken could she get? Netta wondered drearily, and came to the conclusion that marriage was turning her into an accomplished liar. Hastily, she built upon the accidental impression she had conveyed.

'I certainly do,' she murmured, and hated herself for the deception. She touched the cloth of her slacks sentimentally against her cheek. The stones in the belt felt reassuringly hard and lumpy. 'No one washes the stains from a wedding dress, do they?' she asked softly, and blessed the fact that the maid had a romantic streak.

'Of course they don't,' Mary sounded quite indignant. 'And there was me, going to wash out all those memories!'

If only soap and water would wash the memories away. Wash away the whole episode, and return her to the carefree, heartwhole person she was before she went to Lak. She suddenly felt immeasurably older than Mary, although there were only a few years between them. And there was still the problem of where to put her safari suit.

'It'll be perfectly all right in the chest of drawers, until I come back from my bath,' she told herself firmly. The last few weeks had made her ultra-nervous. 'I'm in a private house, not an hotel,' she convinced herself she was over-reacting to strain. There was no danger of anyone touching her safari suit, now she had successfully diverted Mary's attention. Mrs Berry was the only other person likely to have designs on her laundry, and she was busy in the kitchen. 'Just the same, I'll tuck it into a drawer.' She waited until the door closed behind Mary before she chose the bottom drawer of the dressing table, and was vividly reminded of the last time she had hidden something at the back of a drawer. 'There's nothing I can do about the jewel settings now,' she shrugged philosophically. She had salvaged the really valuable part of the jewels, and Ranjit was wealthy enough to stand the loss of the rest. She tested the temperature of the bathwater with an experimental toe.

'Bless Mary, it's just right!'

She gave a sigh of pure bliss, and sank into the relaxing warmth of soft water. She reached out and captured a bottle of shampoo that matched the fresh sweetness of the jasmine soap, and luxuriated in foaming perfume. 'I'll shower off,' she decided at last reluctantly, and pulled the plug from the bath, and wriggled under the hissing cold water that tingled her into a liveliness she had not felt for weeks. The receding bath water gurgled, and the shower sang, and——

'Surely that's someone talking?' She tensed and went still as a low-toned hum came from the bedroom next door. It went on, and she fumbled for the shower switch and reached for a towel. The water in the bath gave a final prolonged sucking gurgle, and went silent, and the strains of, 'Ah, 'tis love, and love alone . . .' rose softly in the ensuing silence.

'It's only Mary come back.' Netta gave a sigh of relief and started to towel her hair dry. 'I'll really have to calm down,' she scolded herself. 'If I keep on like this, I'll soon be a nervous wreck!' It was infinitely soothing to feel the fresh silk of her borrowed undies against her skin, and to lie back in the chair in front of the dressing table and give in to Mary's plea to be allowed to brush her hair.

'Mrs Berry says you need to rest, now you're home.'

'I'll do that a lot better when I know how the people from the Embassy got on.' Joss had not mentioned them, and a sudden fear assailed Netta. Surely he would have told her if he had heard any news of Wendy and Harry Fraser? But he had kept his own counsel on other matters that affected her, so it was just possible he had done the same on this. She bit her lip, torn between anxiety and anger.

'They're all safe, didn't you know?' Mary looked astonished at her ignorance. 'It was in all the papers. Mrs Berry showed it to me. She kept a copy to show to Mr Joss when he got home, I know. There's a picture of him in it, and one of the Ambassador and his wife.'

'We haven't seen any English papers since we left the Embassy,' Netta forestalled the inevitable question of why her own photograph did not accompany that of Joss. Now she knew her friends were safe, she felt free to attend to her own problems....

'That's how we knew you were married in the first place,' Mary prattled on. 'It said as how the Embassy people, and the Lak Royal Family, had landed safely in Italy. Fancy Mr Joss knowing the Lak Royal Family!' she marvelled. 'But they said there was no news of Mr and Mrs de Courcey, and we were that worried. And then, of course, we had Mr Joss's cable from the boat, and that put everything right again.'

It might have put everything right for the staff at Thimbles. So far as she was concerned, it put everything wrong, Netta thought wryly, but all she said aloud was,

'It must have come as a shock to Mrs Berry, to hear the news of our marriage like that.' Not half such a shock as it had been to herself, but she refrained from commenting on that as well.

'Not a lot upsets Mrs Berry,' the young maid twinkled suddenly. 'Though it came as a shock to Miss Caroline, I reckon.' Her voice held a wealth of satisfaction. 'She came hotfoot down here the same morning as the newspapers came out, and then tried to make out she didn't know anything about it. And her with a copy of the *Gazette* in her luggage, and the pictures and the story all over the front page!' The young voice was scornful. So her intuition about Caroline had been correct, Netta thought.

'Miss Caroline doesn't live here permanently, then?' she asked in a disinterested voice.

'Not her,' Mary exclaimed ungrammatically. ''Tisn't smart enough, down here, for her. She'd rather live in London, and have the bright lights.'

'That will be all, Mary. You can go now.'

Netta jumped as Joss's voice spoke from just behind them. I should be used to him by now, she thought vexedly, indignation rising in her on the heels of fright.

'I'll come and clear up in here for you, while you're downstairs having your dinner, Mrs de Courcey.' Mary did not seem at all disconcerted by Joss's silent approach.

'Don't touch my safari suit,' Netta began urgently as Mary made for the door, and she turned back again and replied happily,

'I gave your trouser suit to Mr Joss, ma'am. He came up and asked for it while you were having your bath. He said as how he'd keep it safe for you, since you wanted it as a souvenir.' She beamed at Joss, obviously applauding his sentiment.

'How dare you take possession of my suit?' The anger that smouldered inside Netta spilled over as the door closed behind the maid. It must have been Joss's voice she had heard when she was showering off after her bath. If only she had opened the door into the bedroom and investigated, instead of being content just to listen, she could have prevented him from taking it.

'Where have you put it?' she cried furiously.

'It's in my safe, where it will remain until your father comes home.'

'That might be weeks!' Netta stared at him in disbelief. 'I can take the jewels to the bank on Wednesday, they'll be open then.' Her chin came up. 'I intend to take them to the bank on Wednesday.'

'Since they're in my safe, you won't be able to,' Joss replied with a calm deliberation that served to incense her further. 'It's no good arguing,' his voice hardened as she raised hers in protest, 'I shall hand the jewels over to your father myself. I won't have you wandering around carrying valuables worth half the price of the Crown Jewels,' he told her bluntly. His estimate of their possible value was not far wrong, but Netta was too angry to appreciate his inspired guesswork. 'It isn't safe for a girl to have such things in her possession.' He did not say anything about it being unsafe for a man, she thought bitingly. It was typical of his chauvinistic attitude, she told herself furiously, but before she could speak he went on, 'Anything could happen while you'd got them in your possession, and I intend to have a word with your father as soon as he comes back, about allowing you to act as his courier on such errands,' he added grimly.

'What I do for my father is none of your business,' Netta blazed, goaded out of control by his overbearing attitude. 'I'm over twenty-one, and I'll please myself what I do,' she asserted her independence.

'Before we were married, it wasn't any of my business,' Joss conceded, and she gave a disbelieving hiss. It simply wasn't possible that Joss should admit something was not his concern, she thought sarcastically, and the next minute he spoiled it by adding, 'now you're married to me I intend to make it my business.' And remedy the situation according to his satisfaction, his tone added, and stung her to fury.

'In that case, you can consider us unmarried, as from now.' Netta's self-control snapped, and she struggled to pull the ring from her finger with frantic haste. Her hurry, and her own indulgence in wallowing in the warm bathwater, was her undoing. The ring was a perfect fit to start with, and the warm wetness had slightly swollen her fingers. The slender gold band resisted her hasty tugging, and stubbornly refused to budge.

'I told you before,' Joss caught both her hands in a hard grasp, and pulled her to him with fierce impatience, 'while you're with me, you'll wear my ring.' His voice was tense, his face tight with an anger that matched her own, and he glowered down at her with a look that made her catch her breath. A small detached part of her remembered that when he was angry, tiny deep bronze flecks glowed like living coals deep in the gold of his eyes. They glowed now, and her own eyes faltered before them.

'I brought you to Thimbles as my wife,' he gritted, 'and while you're here you'll observe the conventions.'

'You dragged me to Thimbles against my will, and while I'm here there's one convention I've no intention of observing,' she stormed back.

She felt him go still as her meaning penetrated. It was like the dark, brooding stillness before a mighty storm, bottomlessly silent, yet cracklingly alive with electric currents that might at any second erupt in a lightning sheet of flame, to sear and burn.... For a brief, agonising second his grasp on her hands increased to bone-crushing force, and she pulled away, and opened her mouth to cry out at the pain of his grip, and then could have cried at the even greater pain as he released them, and thrust them away from him as if he hated their touch, so that she found herself pulling against nothing, and staggered backwards against the side of the bed, shaken out of balance by her own momentum. She put out her hands and grasped at the quilt to save herself from falling full length across it, and her stunned mind heard him say coldly,

'I don't force my company on any woman.'

He spun away from her then and strode towards the door. The handle rattled under the force of his grip as he wrenched it open, and the sharp noise kindled Netta into a retort.

'Don't wait for me to follow you down,' she threw at his retreating back. 'Mary can bring my meal up here to me.' He paused, his back still turned, and she rushed on recklessly, 'I'm sure you'll enjoy your tête-à-tête with Caroline much better without my presence!'

He turned, then, and the tightly leashed anger in his face dried the words unspoken on her lips. Instinctively she ran the tip of her tongue across them, her mouth suddenly parched, and a tremor ran through her when he spoke. His words seemed to cut across the room like a lance, and she flinched away from their barb.

'Now you mention Mary,' his look pierced her, refusing to allow her to look away, and she felt like a butterfly fluttering helplessly against a pin, 'you will kindly refrain from questioning the house staff on matters that concern the family.' He did not say 'will you', he said, 'you will', and Netta bridled resentfully at his order. 'If you want any information, ask me,' he commanded her harshly.

'Since you didn't volunteer any information, I'd no option but to ask the servants,' she defended herself hotly. 'And in case you want a full account of my conversation,' she ignored his impatient gesture and rushed on, 'I wasn't questioning Mary about your family, we were discussing a newspaper article that it seems appeared after you and I left Lak, and gave the news that the people in the plane landed safely in Italy. I suppose even you must consider I'm entitled to receive news of my friends?' she demanded with spirit.

'That's exactly what I came upstairs to show you.' He stepped away from the door and came back towards her, digging a folded newspaper from his pocket on the way. 'Mrs Berry gave me a copy of the paper, and as you say you intend to remain upstairs you might as well have it for company.' He slung it on to the bed beside her, and she steeled herself not to move away. It hit the counterpane beside her with a sharp slap, and the sheets fluttered apart where it landed, then settled with a sigh, and automatically she glanced down at the front page.

Two large photographs looked up at her. One was of Wendy and Harry, and the other—she blinked to clear her eyes—the other was a bright, laughing photograph of Joss. Her heart gave a painful wrench. If only she could make him look like that!—carefree, happy, so different from the set, stern face of the Joss she knew. Who had he been looking at, when he laughed like that? she wondered wretchedly. Caroline? He spoke in a clipped voice.

'The meal will be served in the dining room in,' he flicked his shirt cuff back from his wrist, 'in exactly a quarter of an hour. Mary will be serving at table, and she won't have time to bring food upstairs. You can either join me at table, or go hungry.'

And he was gone. With the same swift tread that never ceased to astonish her, and left her no time in which to think of a retort, he closed the door behind him and she was alone, except for the image of his likeness on the counterpane beside her. It gazed up at her from the printed page, and she caught her breath on a sob. Was it her fancy, or did the pictured eyes really seek out her own? Laughing at her. Mocking. . . .

CHAPTER ELEVEN

'I WON'T go downstairs and join Joss. I'll starve first!'

It was easier said than done. Netta flicked through the newspaper in a desultory fashion, and tried in vain to subdue the hollow pleading from inside her that cried out for the waiting meal. And all the time, Joss's eyes seemed to follow her every movement from the photograph on the front page.

'Oh, do stop looking at me!'

In desperation she turned the paper face down and flung it back on the bed.

'I'd better move these dresses, it's a shame to crease them.' Restlessly, she began to sort out the clothes Mary had brought her. Movement brought some small relief from the tension, and she paused as she came to the primrose yellow dress. 'I might as well get dressed,' she decided. 'I can't stay in a robe for the rest of the day.' There was not much of the day left now, but she felt better when she slipped the dress over her head, and found it was a perfect fit, as were the white sandals, she discovered, which the young maid had thoughtfully provided to go with it. She smoothed sheer tights over her legs and eyed herself critically in the mirror. 'Mmm, it's good to be in a dress again!' However much she enjoyed wearing slacks when the occasion demanded, after weeks with nothing else to put on each day but her safari suit, it was a treat to wear something feminine again. Netta frankly enjoyed being a girl, and had every lovely woman's delight in pretty things.

Her own reflection returned a solemn, hazel-eyed stare from the full-length mirror. It showed little, she thought thankfully, of the emotional storm through which she had just passed. Perhaps her eyes were a trifle over-bright, but that could have been the glint of renewed confidence that surged through her as she surveyed her own slender,

primrose-clad figure. Her still damp curls formed a tight
halo round her head, and her flawless skin, that went
with her bright colouring, was becomingly tanned. It was
about the only bonus she had to remind her of her stay
abroad, she thought wryly.

'My, but you do look nice! What a difference a pretty
dress makes.' Mrs Berry's ample reflection appeared beside
her own in the mirror, and the apple-cheeked face beamed
approval. 'I said Miss Rosemary's clothes would be a good
fit for you,' she observed with satisfaction.

'They're lovely, and just the right size.' Netta smiled
back, suddenly glad of the older woman's company. Perhaps—quick hope rose in her—perhaps she might be able
to persuade Mrs Berry to bring her something on a tray.

'I saw Mr Joss go downstairs, so I told him I'd show
you the way to the dining room. He said you weren't going
to bother to dress for dinner, seeing as it's early anyhow,
so what Mary brought you to put on will do nicely,' she
surveyed Netta with open approval. 'Mr Joss persuaded
his cousin to eat with you at the same time, so as to save
me cooking twice. He's considerate that way, is Mr Joss.'
Which implied that Caroline was not, Netta thought, un-
surprised, then her heart sank.

'I can't ask for a tray upstairs now,' she realised des-
pondently. Unwittingly, Mrs Berry had foiled her intentions, and she turned towards the door with reluctant feet.
'I wasn't going to bother to eat,' she began, 'I'm not really
hungry any more.' Her stomach instantly gave a loud wail,
and proclaimed her statement to be a lie.

'You've gone past eating, that's why,' Mrs Berry
clucked her concern. 'Just come down and try a morsel or
two, and you'll find your appetite will come back,' she
promised cheerfully.

'I don't know.' Still Netta hesitated. 'Joss will have
someone to talk to, if Caroline's eating with him.' The
thought of sitting with Caroline at the meal table really did
take away her appetite.

'Aye, I don't doubt she'll enjoy the opportunity,' the
housekeeper answered slyly, and Netta glanced at her

suspiciously. On the face of it, it was a casual enough comment, but.... She made up her mind swiftly.

'I won't give Caroline the satisfaction of driving me away,' she told herself firmly. 'I think, after all, I'll take your advice,' she added aloud, and summoned up a smile, which broadened of its own accord at Mrs Berry's instant nod of satisfaction. She regarded the housekeeper in a new light. Underneath her kindly good humour, she was not above a little guileful manipulation if she wanted to obtain her own way, Netta realised amusedly. The faded eyes twinkled, but Mrs Berry did not say anything until they were half way down the stairs, where she paused, as seemed her habit, to regain her breath.

'That's a picture of the first Jocelyn de Courcey,' she indicated one of the portraits hung at a vantage point above them. 'He's very like our Mr Joss, isn't he?'

'Our Mr Joss....' Netta's heart gave a painful lurch at the housekeeper's choice of words, and then another that made her draw a hard breath as she looked up obediently, and met the gold, painted stare of the man in the portrait. The likeness to Joss was startling. Given that the portrait had been painted nearly six hundred years ago, it could almost have been Joss himself, in fancy dress. The hair was longer, in the fashion of the age, but the same pointed features looked down at her, and the same gold eyes. The long-ago artist had even captured the tiny amber-coloured flecks deep within them.

'They called him the Fox,' Mrs Berry observed, and Netta turned on her a startled look.

'They called Joss that, too, in Lak.'

'They're not the only ones to see the likeness....' Now she knew what he had meant.

'Well, I never!' Mrs Berry resumed her journey, and in deference to her age and bulk Netta slowed her own steps. 'It's the eyes, I expect,' the housekeeper went on chattily. 'Now and then they come out, somewhere in the line. The old Earl had them, but they missed Mr Joss's father, and came down to Mr Joss. It's odd, how these things happen in a family, isn't it?' she mused. 'They miss a generation or two, and then they pop up again, just when you think they've gone for ever.'

'The portrait's in a wonderful state of preservation.' Netta deftly sidetracked the housekeeper. She did not want to let her thoughts dwell on men with gold-coloured eyes. 'The colours are still so bright,' she hurried on, her voice slightly breathless, though not for the same reason as Mrs Berry. 'Even the stones in the ring on his finger look as if they're real.' Her training made her notice them particularly. They glowed richly coloured, one large central ruby, surrounded by diamonds and rubies graded in size, in a richly ornate setting.

'It's a lovely ring,' Mrs Berry agreed amiably. 'The old Earl left it to Miss Caroline. It's the only thing he did leave her,' she added in a dry tone.

And Caroline hoped to remedy what she considered a poor inheritance, by marrying Joss, Netta thought with quick intuition. No wonder the newspaper article had come as such a shock to her!

'Not so loud, girl, not so loud!' Mrs Berry reached the hall and regained breath and voice in shocked protest as Mary sounded the gong with more energy than discretion. 'You're calling folk to eat, not waking the shades,' she scolded.

'Mr Joss is already in the dining room,' Mary volunteered, unabashed. 'Miss Caroline isn't down yet.'

'She won't be able to complain she hasn't heard the gong,' Mrs Berry returned with an asperity that Netta suspected was not entirely directed against the maid, and then she nearly lost her resolution as it dawned on her what Mary had just said.

Joss was already in the dining room. Alone. And although she did not relish the thought of Caroline's company, her courage failed her at the prospect of facing Joss on his own.

'I'll come in with you for a minute,' Mrs Berry prevented her from giving way to cowardice, and running back to her room—their room.... She forced herself to listen to what the housekeeper was saying. Anything, to still the sudden wild beating of her heart as she approached the dining room door.

'I just want to check that Mary's laid the table properly,' Mrs Berry fussed. 'She's a good girl, and coming along nicely, but now and then she forgets.' She opened the door and bustled into the room, and straight away made for the small circular table placed in front of the open french windows. The snowy cloth and gleaming silver looked inviting in the evening sunlight, but Netta hardly noticed them. She paused in the doorway, and her eyes were drawn across the room as if by a magnet, straight to Joss. He leaned easily against the fireplace. He, too, had changed into casual clothes, a cream silk shirt which he had left open at the neck so that it showed the strong, dark column of his throat, and dark chocolate-coloured slacks that made him seem even taller and slimmer than before. He must have showered, too, she noticed with a detached kind of interest that his hair was still damp, like her own.

He looked up, and their glances met and locked across the room. Her heart stopped its wild beating. For a brief, electrifying second, it seemed to stop beating altogether.

'It's only because I'm hungry,' she told herself desperately. But hunger could not be responsible for the strange paralysis that kept her rooted to the spot in the doorway, unable to move, scarcely able to breathe.

'Mary can start serving right away, Mrs Berry.' After what seemed an aeon of time his eyes left her—released her—and she drew a deep, shuddering breath. 'You'll sit here, beside me.' With his silent, lithe tread he crossed the room and stood over her. He reached down and took her elbow, and she quivered at his touch, but she did not, could not, draw away. In spite of the warmth of the evening she felt icily cold, and she shivered. She felt him look down at her, as if the shiver had communicated itself to him, but she did not look up. She could not—dared not—meet his eyes again. Somehow, her legs carried her beside him to the table, though she felt herself walk woodenly, like a doll without joints, and it was with an infinite sense of re-

lief that she collapsed, rather than sat, on the chair he drew
out for her.

'Miss Caroline isn't down yet, Mr Joss.' Mrs Berry
hesitated by the door.

'She won't be long,' Joss answered absently, 'she's just
gone upstairs to change her dress.'

'I had to, after Tara scraped her paws all down the
front of the other one, and spoiled it.' Caroline appeared
and darted a spiteful look in Netta's direction. 'It wouldn't
have happened if the dog had been left where she was
until Joss called her,' she added critically, and Netta gripped her hands together under the cover of the table cloth.

'I won't quarrel with her,' she resolved firmly. 'I'm only
here for a day or two, so it isn't worth it,' only to have her
good intentions nearly fail her as Caroline added,

'You can start serving now, Mrs Berry.'

'I should be giving the instructions, not Caroline.' The
thought caught Netta by surprise. It should not matter to
her, since she did not intend to remain, either at Thimbles,
or as Joss's wife. But she found, unexpectedly, that it did
matter. It angered her unaccountably. Caroline was deliberately usurping her place as Joss's wife. It was she who
was the guest in the house, not Netta. She was not to
know that Joss's marriage was merely one of convenience.
Or had Joss told her, while they talked together in the
drawing room? The possibility gave her pause, and increased her anger against both Joss and Caroline. He had
no right to discuss their marriage with anyone. It was
something that belonged to them alone. To bring a third
person in, particularly if that person was Caroline, seemed
like trampling over sacred ground, and her resentment increased accordingly.

'Come and sit this side of me,' Joss performed the same
courtesy for his cousin, and held her chair until she sat
down.

'Not so far away, darling.' She immediately edged it
closer to his. 'You've been too far away for too long. Do be
careful, Mary!' she broke off and rebuked the young maid
sharply, careless of the fact that it was her own action

which had caught the girl's elbow and hazarded the dishes in her hand. Her move nearer to Joss had made it difficult for the maid to serve properly, and Netta had a moment's irresponsible hope that if anything spilled as a consequence, it might do so over Caroline.

'It's not like me to be catty.' She took a tight hold of her thoughts, and smiled encouragingly at Mary, and was rewarded as the girl's face brightened and she continued to serve with renewed confidence.

'I wish we'd gone to a restaurant for our meal.' Netta concentrated on her soup, and tried to think of something to say. Mrs Berry's cooking certainly lived up to Mary's recommendation, she thought appreciatively, but it was spoiled for her by the currents of tension and antagonism that loaded the sun-filled air across the table. If Caroline felt the atmosphere, she gave no sign, though most of it emanated from her. She kept up a running flow of small talk, mostly directed at Joss about people and places they both knew, and which, Netta did not doubt, was specifically designed to exclude herself, although now and then Caroline seemed to recollect herself, and directed a remark to Netta which she noticed each time did not require a reply. The effect was to give Caroline the appearance of a gracious hostess expertly coping with a difficult and rather gauche guest, and Netta seethed inwardly as the meal progressed.

'She manages to look the part,' she conceded grudgingly. Caroline had changed into a short black dress as severely cut as her green linen, but in a softer, more becoming material. It acted as a perfect foil for her upswept hair, and made Netta's simple summer primrose seem childish by comparison. The inference was obvious, at least to Netta. Caroline was trying to impress upon Joss, without actually saying so in so many words, what a mistake he had made in marrying Netta—and how much better Caroline herself would fulfil the role of chatelaine at Thimbles. It was cleverly done. Netta could even guess at the phrases Caroline would employ to her friends, to explain the situation.

'Some little ingénue Joss picked up abroad. They were both caught up in the uprising in Lak. Men do quixotic things at such times. A moment of madness....' And then the punch line. 'Fortunately, such moments aren't irreparable, these days.'

She became aware of a waiting sort of silence, and looked up. Caroline and Joss were both looking at her, as if they expected her to say something.

'I didn't catch....' she began, guiltily conscious that she had shut her ears to Caroline's chatter, and become totally absorbed in her own thoughts. It rankled that her own inattention had put her at a disadvantage.

'Caroline was suggesting we might hold a ball at Thimbles,' Joss broke the strained silence, and his voice held more than a hint of impatience.

'I suggested a party, darling,' Caroline corrected him prettily, 'but of course if you'll agree to a ball....' Her face brightened. 'It's time Thimbles saw a bit of life again. We could have a ball right away, to celebrate your homecoming.' She did not say, celebrate *their* homecoming, Netta noticed, nor suggest celebrating the fact that she and Joss were married. Perhaps Joss had told her that there was nothing to celebrate in that connection.

'And then we could have the Hunt Ball here, at the end of the season,' the other girl planned ahead enthusiastically, and Netta looked across at her speculatively. Surely Hunt Balls took place after Christmas? She counted up the months, aware of a growing feeling of dismay. How long did Caroline intend to remain at Thimbles? It should not concern her, because she herself would not be here, but.... She checked her thoughts hastily and forced herself to pay attention to what Joss was saying. She did not want to give Caroline the satisfaction of attracting his criticism again.

'Not the Hunt Ball. Not at Thimbles.' Surprisingly, he refused his cousin, and Netta looked at him questioningly. There seemed to be an underlying something in his tone which she did not understand. From her reaction it was evident that Caroline did.

'Oh, darling, don't say you're going to carry on all those old prejudices,' she protested. 'I thought all that had died with the Earl.'

'My uncle didn't consider them to be prejudices,' Joss answered her quietly, 'and neither do I.'

'Just because of a silly old family crest?' Caroline scoffed, but Netta noticed that her gracious air was beginning to fray slightly at the unexpected opposition. 'It's only a picture,' she persisted, 'even if it is carved in stone, or whatever.'

'It was more than a picture to my ancestor,' Joss pointed out in a mild tone, and Netta looked at him sharply. That was twice he had said it. 'My uncle', and then, 'my ancestor'. Not 'our uncle—our ancestor', which suggested that his relationship with Caroline was not a particularly close one by blood. He had called her his cousin, but it could be that she was a second or third time removed. Which, and Netta's heart gave a painful twist at the thought, which would make marriage a more acceptable proposition between them, if their blood tie was only a distant one.

'Oh, that!' Caroline began to sound impatient in her turn. 'Just because the first Jocelyn de Courcey happened to be nicknamed the Fox—goodness knows why.' Netta knew, but if Caroline could not see the simile in the pointed face and the strange golden eyes, there was little use in anyone trying to tell her, she thought.

'It was the reason the first Jocelyn included the animal in his crest,' Joss pointed out reasonably, and Netta listened with interest. She had noticed the crest carved in stone over the main doorway when they arrived. There was a small replica of it in the stone of the mantel over the fire-place in the room they now occupied. It consisted of crossed swords supporting an open book, and surrounded by a wreath of wheat ears, symbolising a soldier, a scholar, and a landowner, the whole surmounted by his own particular monogram of a fox's mask. The shield was still peculiarly applicable to the present owner of Thimbles, Netta thought, and became aware that he was still speak-

ing. His voice remained mild, but it had in it an under-
tone of inflexible determination that she had heard herself
on more than one occasion, though for some reason she
felt surprised that he applied it to Caroline.

'The first Jocelyn's nickname, and his crest, were the
reasons why he refused to have the fox hunted on his land.
He knew what it felt like himself, to be hunted,' Joss
added reflectively.

And so did Joss. And, for that matter, so did she, Netta
thought ruefully. A vision of the rebels fanning the flames
among the scrub, in the hope of flushing them both out
of hiding, rose vividly in her mind's eye, and for a brief,
revealing second she turned her head and looked straight at
Joss, and knew that his thoughts were following her own.
It gave her a momentary feeling of closeness with him, the
shared terror, and the shared escape, and all that went between. She must not think of all that went between. She
drew a long breath and sat up straight in her chair, and
with an effort kept her mind from wandering, even though
she did not particularly want to listen to what Caroline was
saying. The latter unwisely continued to protest.

'Surely you can't be serious, Joss? If you carry that kind
of outlook to its conclusion, you'll stop crop shooting next.
And where will you be then? Overrun with rabbits,' she
concluded triumphantly.

'Since I intend to leave the foxes to breed freely on
Thimbles land, they'll keep the rabbit population in check
for me,' Joss returned amusedly, but his eyes held a hint of
steel that his cousin must have caught, because she
shrugged and gave a light laugh, and waved a deprecating
hand.

'Oh well, it's your land,' she conceded. 'Perhaps one day
I can persuade you to change your mind.'

'I wish you luck, if you try to make him change it,'
Netta thought with an inward flash of humour of her own,
and found her eyes caught by the glint of jewels on
Caroline's finger as the girl cupped her hands round her
face and regarded Joss indulgently, as if she was temporarily giving way to what she regarded as a harmless

whim, that she would talk him out of later. Surely—Netta looked at her hand more keenly—surely it was the same ring as the one she had seen in the painting on the stairs?

'That belonged to the first Jocelyn de Courcey.' Joss caught her glance, and firmly directed the conversation into another channel.

'I noticed it on the painting as I came downstairs,' Netta followed his lead with relief. Perhaps now she would be able to join in the conversation, instead of Caroline monopolising both it and Joss, she thought tartly.

'How very observant of you,' the other girl sneered, but Joss did not seem to notice her sarcasm, and went on conversationally,

'It's not really so very remarkable,' he pointed out. 'Netta's a jeweller by profession. Her father is John Vaughan, the jeweller and goldsmith.'

Did she imagine it? Netta wondered, or did a wary look creep into Caroline's eyes as he mentioned the renowned name? She dismissed it as nothing but fancy, and made another effort to help the conversation along.

'It's a lovely ring,' she tried holding out an olive branch. Few women could resist having their jewellery praised, and if it made the atmosphere between them a little easier it would be worth it, she thought cynically. 'I see you've resorted to the same safety measure as a lot of our clients,' she gave the ring a professional glance, 'so many people nowadays are having the real stones replaced by synthetics, and keeping the originals in the bank.' She tried not to let her own regret show through. 'It's a sensible idea, and so much safer than wearing the originals.'

'How dare you suggest the stones are synthetic?' Caroline's outburst startled her. It could not possibly have been assumed. The girl's face went white with fury, and she glared at Netta balefully across the table. With a swift movement she drew her hands away from her face, which effectively removed the ring from view. 'You come here as a complete outsider,' she ignored the fact that Joss had brought her as his wife, 'and within minutes you're responsible for spoiling my dress, and now you have the impertinence to suggest my ring isn't genuine! It's a family heirloom,' she stormed, the last vestiges of her gracious behaviour vanished, and naked hostility burning in her pale blue eyes. 'What right have you got to say such a thing?' she demanded hotly. 'You've scarcely set eyes on the ring.'

'I haven't had a close look at it,' Netta began, completely taken aback by the other girl's verbal attack. She did not need to look at the ring closely. When Caroline had leaned on the table, her finger had been less than a couple of feet away, and Netta possessed excellent eyesight, and a professional judgment equal to that of her father where gemstones were concerned.

'There, you see?' Caroline appealed to Joss. 'She's just saying that, to try to make trouble.'

'Even professionals can be mistaken.' To Netta's amazement, Joss took his cousin's side without hesitation, and the look he directed at herself was both angry and impatient. 'Netta will acknowledge that, and apologise,' he added sternly, his eyes accusing her of deliberately upsetting his first evening back in his own home. Netta gasped at the injustice of his attitude. He was as bad as Caroline, she thought furiously. Worse. As her husband, he should have taken her side, or at least listened to her point of view. She felt as if she was on one side of a high door, hammering for admission, with Joss and Caroline both on the other side, keeping it firmly shut against her.

'I'm sure it can be sorted out amicably.' Joss paused significantly, evidently waiting for Netta to make the desired apology.

'In that case, you must do the sorting yourself,' she declared mutinously, and rose from her chair with a swift angry movement. She felt a moment's irreverent thankfulness that she had managed to eat a good part of the meal before the outbreak of hostilities; it would have been difficult to make a dignified exit if her hunger had remained unsatisfied. As it was,

'I've never had to apologise for a professional judgment yet, and I don't intend to do so now,' she informed Joss with quiet dignity. 'If you doubt my word,' she spoke coldly to Caroline, 'I suggest you have your ring valued. You'll find your insurance premium will be drastically reduced,' she told the other girl confidently, and added in a biting tone, 'that is, if you've got it insured in the first place.'

She did not wait to see the effect of her words on either Caroline or Joss. As she finished speaking, the dining room door opened to admit Mary with the trolley, and the presence of the maid effectively precluded any further conversation while she was in the room. Netta took advantage of the interruption to slip through the door and make good her escape upstairs. Her heart was hammering in agitated protest at the sheer unreasonableness of Joss's attitude, but despite her upset feelings she nevertheless paused in her hasty flight as she reached the oil painting, and gave it a closer scrutiny. She had not been mistaken about the ring. The painting confirmed what she already knew. She recommenced her ascent with slower steps, and shrugged. It was not her business. Caroline owned the piece of jewellery, and what she did with it was her own affair, but Netta's sense of justice smarted under Joss's criticism, as affronted as was her professional pride by his open expression of doubt.

'The sooner I'm back in London, and working again, the happier I'll be,' she told herself, and knew it was not true. To do her work properly, her heart had to be in it—and her heart refused to be parted from Joss. It beat wildly when he finally appeared through the bedroom door over an hour later, that seemed like a million years of waiting to Netta. She picked up the newspaper from where she had thrown it on the counterpane, and looked again at his photograph, then turned it back face downwards again on the bed, because she was unable to bear the knowledge that his smile was not for her. Unable to bear to be without it, so that she turned it back again, then found she could not see it properly, because her eyes were blurred with tears. She wiped them hastily as the door handle rattled and he strode into the room.

'I'll apologise to Caroline, if it's only to keep the peace,' she decided miserably as the door opened, then had her weakening resolution tossed to the winds by Joss's very first words as he came towards her across the room.

'Did you *have* to provoke an argument with Caroline over her ring?' he demanded angrily, and the deep amber flecks glowed like coals in his eyes. 'I've been until now trying to calm her down.' He evidently did not think it important to try and calm Netta, and anger rose in her again at his unfair discrimination, but he went on before she could speak, 'She was trying her utmost to be pleasant to you all during dinner, and you scarcely spoke a word until this upset started. You might at least have met her half way. Just because you've got red hair, you don't need to start a battle with everyone in sight....'

'For heaven's sake!' She jumped to her feet, her temper flaring in her own defence. 'If you think Caroline was trying to be pleasant to me, you know very little about women,' she told him scornfully. 'And my hair isn't red, it's auburn.' She was too angry to notice the slight twitch to his lips as she said it, and it was gone immediately as she stormed on, 'I didn't provoke any argument with Caroline. I made the mistake of trying to join in the conversation, instead of allowing her to monopolise it, that's all. How was I to know she'd flare up like that over her beastly ring?' she demanded passionately.

'It's enough to make any woman flare up, when the authenticity of her jewellery is put into question,' Joss observed drily.

'I wasn't questioning it,' Netta denied flatly. 'I was stating a fact.'

'What possible proof have you got?' Joss began, and she interrupted him impatiently.

'I don't need proof.' She faced him squarely. 'My own knowledge of jewellery is quite sufficient.' Her voice rang with conviction. She was sure of her ground on this score, at least, and wished it gave her some satisfaction. 'But of course, if you'd prefer not to listen to me,' she said coldly.

'Go on—tell me.' The stern look on Joss's face did not

relax, and she spoke defensively. There was no reason why she should shield Caroline, and since it was not Joss's ring, it was not his business either, she decided with a mental shrug.

'Wendy told me your family went back to Agincourt, which would be the first Jocelyn de Courcey—the one in the painting on the stairs?' Joss nodded, but he did not speak, and she took a deep breath and went on, 'The portrait shows him as a young man in soldier's dress, wearing the ring. Presumably that was after Agincourt. The battle was fought in 1415, and I imagine the portrait was painted when he returned, to hang in the house he built here?'

'You're remarkably accurate so far.' Joss's voice was expressionless. 'Go on guessing,' he invited.

'It's deduction, not guesswork,' Netta replied coldly. 'One look at the ring told me enough to know that who-ever put the synthetic stones in it,' she saw Joss's face tighten, but she went on uncaring, rubbing in her point with angry emphasis, 'whoever replaced the real stones made the mistake of, putting it crudely, trying to "tart up" the ring.'

'In what way?' Still his face remained tight, but she sensed she had at least gained his attention.

'By cutting the stones with facets,' Netta mustered her patience to explain as simply as she could. 'Until the fifteenth century, stones were not cut with facets. They were used solely for their colour. I imagine the ring worn by your ancestor was fairly old, even when he acquired it?' she raised questioning eyebrows, and Joss nodded.

'It was bestowed as a gift for valour. He returned with it from France.' He confirmed her judgment, and it gave her renewed confidence to continue.

'Synthetic stones have to be cut and polished in exactly the same manner as natural gems, and whoever cut the stones in the present ring did so by using what we call, in the trade, the brilliant cut. That didn't come in until round about 1700, it's got fifty-eight facets, and it's used to reflect and refract light, which gives the stones, particularly diamonds, the brilliant sparkle we're used to now. That sparkle alone told me the gems had been tampered with, even though the setting itself is obviously old, probably the original one.'

'Anything else?' Joss queried, and Netta looked at him, suspicious of sarcasm, but his face revealed nothing, and she went on thoughtfully,

'There's one other thing, though it wouldn't point to the ruby being necessarily synthetic,' she conceded. 'But from where I sat, the principal stone looked to be absolutely flawless. I couldn't be sure without a closer examination, but it isn't often one gets a natural, completely flawless gem of such a size. It could be confirmed by a test,' she went on, 'and if such a large ruby were indeed flawless, it would be virtually priceless as well, so if Caroline's right and I'm wrong, she'd be well advised to make sure her ring's insured,' she added drily, and her tone said she was confident of her own facts, and at the same time doubted if the ring would be insured, adequately or otherwise. 'My father's got a testing kit in our lab at home,' she offered, 'or,' and her voice held a thin edge of sarcasm, 'or if Caroline doesn't trust us, she could always take the ring to the London Chamber of Commerce laboratory, they'd test it for her there. But I've no doubt they'd confirm everything I say,' she said with spirited conviction, 'which is why I've got no intention of apologising to her,' she finished defiantly.

CHAPTER TWELVE

'You could at least come downstairs and attempt to make it up,' Joss said shortly, and Netta stared at him in amazement.

'Make up what?' she demanded angrily. 'I didn't quarrel with Caroline, she quarrelled with me. And if there's any making up, or apologising, to be done, it's her place to do it,' she declared stormily. 'Besides, I'm tired,' she added. 'It's been a long day, and I've got no intention of coming downstairs again tonight.' That at least was true, she thought dispiritedly, a cloud of weariness caught up with her and she suddenly felt limp, although she suspected that most of it was caused by nervous tension rather than by actual tiredness. With an effort she rallied her energies. Now was not the time to give in.

'There's another thing,' she said, before Joss had time to speak. If grievances were going to be aired, she decided, she might as well do her share, instead of sitting back meekly and letting Caroline and Joss toss all the arrows in her direction. 'Your cousin behaves as if I don't exist,' she complained bitterly. 'It's true,' she insisted, as he opened his mouth to speak. 'She's planning parties, right into next year, and she speaks to the servants as if it's she who's mistress here. For that matter, why is she here?' she demanded to know. 'And how long is she going to stay? She's acting as if she intends to make it her permanent home, and she's behaving as if I'm the guest in the house, instead of herself. You married me to solve your own difficulties,' she accused him bitterly, 'but I'm still entitled to be treated....'

'Caroline came here for the same reason as you did yourself, because her house in London is in the throes of redecoration, and she didn't want to stay in an hotel,' Joss interrupted her curtly. 'And as for entitlements,' he went on harshly, 'you can't have those without the obligations that go with them. You can't have it both ways, Netta.' He looked at her squarely, and she flinched away from the message in his eyes. 'You've got to make the choice,' he reminded her. 'You seem to have abdicated from your obligations,' his bitterness of tone matched her own, 'and regarding entitlements, surely I should be the one to complain about lack of those? Oh, you needn't worry,' as her eyes widened, 'I won't disturb you. You can sleep in blissful solitude,' he told her cuttingly. 'I'll use my dressing room.'

'Perhaps you'd prefer to go to Caroline?'

She did not know what made her say it. The moment they were uttered, she wished the words unsaid, but it was too late. He had heard them, and his face went white under his tan, and she drew a sharp breath of fear. He spoke, and she shivered at the ice in his voice.

'I'm married to you, not to Caroline,' he reminded her silkily. Did he mean, 'Not to Caroline—yet?' She could not be sure, and he gave her no time to surmise. He continued in a tight voice, 'Since you won't come downstairs, I might as well bid you goodnight now.'

She thought he would turn and go, then, and leave her alone. She did not expect him to turn towards her. She tried to back away, but only succeeded in backing into the bedpost. It was hard, and unyielding—as hard and unyielding as Joss's arm, that went round her and pulled her close against him in a vice-like grip.

'Goodnight, Netta,' he gritted, and bent his head over her. She twisted her head to one side, trying to avoid him, but his other hand came up and caught her under her chin, and turned her face back towards him, tilting it upwards to meet his lips. They descended with a hard, angry pressure, forcing hers apart. They hurt, but the pain was as nothing compared to the agony of knowing that it was anger and not love that drove him. There was no gentleness, no desire, only fury and a fierce urge to retaliate. His kiss went on and on, it felt as if for ever, denying her breath, draining her strength, until she began to feel as if he would never release her. When at last he did, she swayed, half fainting, away from him. She drew in her breath in short, sobbing gasps, and her voice, when she found the strength to use it, came as a thin whimper of sound, scarcely audible as she forced the words through bruised and throbbing lips.

'I hate you....'

She reached back shaking hands and grasped at the bed-post for support.

'Go away ... go....' she gasped. If he did not leave her soon, she would surely collapse. Her legs would not support her, and she clung to the bedpost with the strength of desperation, feeling her senses begin to slip away. Joss's face wavered and became blurred in front of her eyes, and the room began to grow dim.

'Leave me,' she implored. She must not faint in front of him. She must not let him see her weakness. Through a rapidly darkening haze she heard him speak, and the icy fury in his voice acted as an astringent on her failing senses.

'I'm going—and glad to,' he flung at her cuttingly. 'Goodnight, Netta.' And he was gone. She did not see him go. She heard the door slam behind him, but her eyes were closed, although the delicately veined lids could not hold back the welling tears that would no longer be denied, and poured like rain across her cheeks as her nerveless hands loosed their weak hold on the bedpost and she slid helplessly to her knees on the soft sheepskin rug on the floor.

She was back on the cargo vessel. She had to be. There could be no other reason why she still felt seasick. A wave of nausea gripped her, and she opened her eyes and struggled upright against the pillows—and became aware that she was in a bed, not in a bunk. The big double bed in the master suite at Thimbles, that was made up for two. She reached across for the second pillow. It lay in its embroidered case of pristine freshness, uncreased and, she winced, obviously unused. With what seemed a mighty effort she managed to drag it on top of her own pillow, and lay back against the pile with a sigh of relief.

Vaguely she remembered getting into bed the previous

night, but she could not recall what time it was when she finally pulled herself upright off the rug, and with the last vestige of strength crawled between the sheets. Somehow she must have managed to get undressed first. A glance downwards confirmed that she was wearing Rosemary's nightdress, the daisy-sprigged one that went with the robe. She wriggled uneasily, and reached behind to pull the second pillow further down under her shoulders. Her own pillow felt uncomfortably damp and, she stroked her face with cautious fingers, her cheeks felt sore as a consequence. So did her eyes. Listlessly she dropped her hands, and hoped Rosemary also kept some spare make-up in the bathroom cabinet. When she went downstairs to face Joss and Caroline she would need something to disguise the ravages of her distress of the night before.

'Ah, you're awake.' A light tap on the bedroom door was followed by Mrs Berry's beaming face above a silver tray, on which reposed a dainty china morning tea-set and a plate of biscuits.

'It can't be breakfast time yet?' Netta sat up hastily. 'Oh, my goodness!' she groaned, and subsided back on to her pillows, her face as pale as the linen behind her.

'Whatever's the matter?' Mrs Berry's kindly visage was full of concern, and she put the tray hurriedly on the bedside table and took both Netta's hands in her own.

'I don't seem to have got rid of the seasickness from the voyage over.' Netta closed her eyes, and waited for the wave of nausea and giddiness to pass.

'Drink your tea and have a biscuit,' Mrs Berry loosed her hands, and the clink of china, and an inviting pouring-out sound, brought Netta's eyes open again.

'I'd love a cup of tea, but I don't want anything to eat,' she shuddered.

'Just a nibble, you'll find it'll help,' Mrs Berry insisted. 'They're only plain arrowroots, there's nothing to hurt you in these,' as Netta still hesitated.

'It's only the aftermath of seasickness, that's all.' Amusement stirred in Netta as she took the cup and the plate with two crisp round wafers on it. 'It's not....' She stopped, and the amusement died within her. She could not be sure. And seasickness did not normally continue after docking. In fact, she had been free from it for several days before they docked, once the storms subsided. She shivered, suddenly cold, and took a hasty gulp of her tea. It was hot and sweet, and to her surprise it did as Mrs Berry had predicted. She began to feel better immediately.

'There now, that's brought some colour back to your cheeks.' The housekeeper eyed her keenly as she finished the cup. 'You're tired out,' she told Netta. 'You just take your time, and finish your tea and biscuits.'

'I'll get up for breakfast.' Joss had refused to allow her to have her dinner brought up the evening before, and she determined she would not ask again. 'What time?' she began.

'Just whenever you're ready,' Mrs Berry said accommodatingly. 'Mr Joss and Miss Caroline had their breakfast early, and went out riding. Mr Joss said to let you sleep on, so I didn't disturb you.'

He would, Netta thought irascibly, but not for any reasons of consideration, as Mrs Berry supposed. It would be convenient for him, if she slept on. It would give him a watertight excuse to enjoy Caroline's company, without being hampered by her own presence, she thought bitterly.

She slid out of bed cautiously, and tried her legs, then gave a sigh of relief as she stood up without the giddiness and nausea returning. Her legs felt strong enough, she walked a few steps experimentally, her confidence flooding back as they performed with their normal agility.

'It was nothing but hunger,' she told herself robustly. 'I'd been all day without food yesterday, and thanks to Caroline I didn't wait to finish my dinner last night. I've been worrying over nothing.'

In a more cheerful frame of mind she donned a summer skirt and top that Mary produced for her, and ran downstairs to tackle Mrs Berry's substantial breakfast with more zest than she would have believed herself capable of an hour ago.

'I think I'll go for a stroll, it's a lovely morning,' she

decided as the housekeeper came to clear away the table.
'Perhaps I'll take Tara with me, if she'll come,' she smiled
as a russet head appeared round the breakfast room door,
with a wary eye on Mrs Berry. As Joss had seen fit to leave
her to her own devices, she would be glad of the dog's
company.

'Just try and stop her,' Mrs Berry laughed. 'She's been
bothering me to let her in here ever since she heard your
voice when you came downstairs, but I reckoned you were
entitled to eat your meal in peace, so I shut her in the
kitchen until you'd finished.'

'I'm free now, so let's go.' Netta held out her hands to
the dog, which responded with an eagerly waving tail, its
lovely feathering acting like a soft fan and setting up a cool
draught against her legs. 'Which way shall we go?' she
murmured as they reached the steps outside the front door
together, but the setter knew no such indecision. With a
backwards look that clearly invited Netta to follow her, she
trotted off in the direction of the stable block.

'It's easy to see where your favourite haunts lie,' Netta
smiled, but for want of any better direction to follow she
strolled slowly in the wake of the setter. The sun was
pleasantly warm, promising heat as it rose higher. It would
have been nice to go riding while the air was still fresh, she
thought wistfully, and thrust down a wish that Joss might
have roused her to go with him, or even waited for her. But
he had chosen to ride with Caroline instead.

Netta shrugged. There was nothing she could do about
it now, and at least she had Tara for company. Or had she?
She had become so absorbed in her own thoughts that she
had not noticed the setter disappear. She looked round.
The dog was nowhere in sight, but an open door in the
middle of the stable block gave her a clue, and as she
turned towards it, a broad country voice raised in good-
humoured protest confirmed her guess as to her quarry's
whereabouts.

'Leave my brushes alone, will you, you young limb!
They're to groom the horses with, not to play with. Hey,
come back!'

Sounds of a scuffle preceded the setter's reappearance through the stable door. She hurtled into the yard in full flight, swinging a big oval brush in her teeth by its webbing hand strap, then frisked across the gravel and dropped her trophy at Netta's feet with a gruff invitation to play.

'I'll skin you, that I will!' From Tara's reaction, it was evidently a morning ritual which she thoroughly enjoyed. She danced expectantly round the owner of the voice as he thrust the door wide open, and she noticed he carried a ball in one gnarled hand. 'Have this instead,' he invited the setter, 'and let me have my brush back.'

With a strength and accuracy that made Netta exclaim, 'You must be a cricketer!' the newcomer lobbed the ball half way across the paddock that backed on to the stable block, and the dog took off after it like a russet streak.

'The gate. . . .' Netta held her breath. A high five-barred gate guarded the paddock, and it did not seem possible that the dog could stop in time.

'She'll climb that, never fear, ma'am.' The setter did not hesitate. She made straight for it, and went up and over the barrier with the agility of a cat, and Netta let out her breath with relief.

'You'd better have your brush, before she comes back,' she handed it over with a smile.

'She'll not touch it again,' the man said confidently, 'she only grabs it first thing in the morning, just to start the day off, so to speak. Just to let me know she's around.'

'You must be . . .?'

'Will Dyer, ma'am.' He smiled back, and his face creased in a thousand tiny wrinkles, like a friendly prune. He must at one time have been fairly tall, Netta judged, but a life on horseback had bandied his legs, and reduced him much nearer to Netta's own height, but his clear, young-looking eyes belied his bald head, and he obviously took her observation as a compliment.

'You're right about the cricket, Mrs de Courcey.' Netta caught her breath and wished, not for the first time, that her heart would not behave so unsteadily each time someone called her by her married name. But at least the effect did not show, she consoled herself, because Will went on cheerfully, 'I play for the Long Minton team. So does Mr Joss, he's the captain, though we've had to do without him up to now, this summer. I reckon he'll be around a bit more from now on, though?' with a quizzical look at Netta.

'Perhaps.' It was not a question she was in a position to answer. She could only speak for herself, and she did not intend to be around for very long. And afterwards, if Joss married Caroline.... Her heart contracted in a sharp thrust of agony at the thought, and this time it must have shown, because the groom glanced at her keenly.

'You look a bit peaky,' he began, and Netta gave a rather shaky laugh.

'We had a bad journey across on the boat, and I still haven't quite found my land legs yet,' she explained hurriedly. 'It was a cargo ship, and a bit unsteady, and I'm not a very good sailor at the best of times,' she excused herself.

'Come and sit in the stable with me for a minute, the sun's a bit warm out here,' the groom suggested considerately. 'Don't worry about Tara,' he added, as Netta hesitated, glancing towards the paddock, 'she'll hunt rabbits in the hedges for a while before she brings her ball back. She always does.'

He led the way into the stable. It was blessedly cool, and smelt sweetly of hay, and the pleasant, musty aroma of fresh straw. Will pulled up a clean straw bale and motioned to Netta to sit down. 'Rest in the cool for a while,' he suggested kindly.

'Do you mind if I watch?' Netta sat down and eyed the palomino mare on which he had evidently been working when Tara interrupted him.

'Watch away,' Will answered goodhumouredly. 'I can see you like horses,' he discovered the link between them with evident pleasure.

'She's beautiful. It's a long time since I've been able to go riding.' She realised now how much she missed it. Her eyes roamed admiringly over the pale golden mare, her

cream mane and tail like silk, evidence of the groom's
patient care.

'Aye, she's Mr Joss's favourite, is Fleet.' The proud
head turned at the mention of her name, and Netta fondled
the soft muzzle that was thrust enquiringly into her out-
stretched hands.

'Yet Joss isn't riding her?' It seemed strange, if the mare
was his favourite.

'She's in foal, ma'am.' Will stopped his tuneless whistle
to answer her, and his hands stilled for a moment from his
rhythmic brushing. 'She'll need peace and quiet, and a bit
of coddling for a while, won't you, old girl? We've got
the other two mares to cope with any riding Mr Joss wants
to do, while Fleet's out of action.' He resumed grooming,
and Netta relaxed as she watched him. She found the time-
less occupation peculiarly soothing to watch. Men had
been performing the same task from the time they first
gentled horses to do their bidding, and hands would still
be so occupied as long as men and horses remained. There
was no doubt that under Will's hands the palomino would
be carefully tended. 'Coddled,' he had said. She smiled as
she watched him, and knew a quick stab of envy for the
mare. The palomino would have her foal, calm in the
security of familiar surroundings lavished with care that
only love can give. . . .

'Stop it!' she begged her mind, aghast at the trend of
her own thoughts, and turned with relief as Tara bundled
through the door and headed straight for her, to drop the
ball in her lap.

'She's taken to you,' Will commented with a smile, and
Netta rubbed the setter's soft ears.

'It's mutual,' she answered, and stood up. 'I'll take her
ball into the paddock, out of your way.' She paused as the
crisp clop of hooves sounded on the gravel outside.

'Sounds like Mr Joss is back,' Will commented, but
Netta did not stop to listen.

'Come on, Tara!' She snapped her fingers to the setter,
and started hurriedly towards the door. If she was quick,
she might be able to slip away without Joss seeing her.

'I'm a coward,' she told herself scornfully, but her heart failed her at the prospect of meeting him. She reached the door with the setter at her heels, and stopped irresolutely. Another minute and she would have made her escape undetected. But the minute was gone beyond recall, and the two riders were already approaching the stables. Tara gruffed a welcome, and destroyed any hope she might have had of slipping away without Joss seeing her. His eyes levelled with her own across the stable yard, and she felt her throat go dry. It flashed across her mind that the two cousins made a handsome couple. Joss's horse was a dark chestnut. The animal was tall, and Netta surveyed it with knowledgeable eyes; it was a full sixteen hands, if not more, and man and beast made a superb study in bronze against the clear morning light.

'I'll take over the horses for you, Mr Joss.' Will appeared in the stable doorway leading the palomino, and perforce Netta had to step right outside in order to allow him past.

'Thanks, Will.' Joss swung lightly out of the saddle, and turned immediately to help his cousin to dismount. Instead of reaching ground in the orthodox manner, Caroline kicked her feet free from the stirrups and swung her legs across the horse's back, then slid down straight into Joss's arms, where she remained for an unnecessarily long time, Netta thought sourly, laughing up into Joss's face. Watching the two together, a strange feeling took possession of Netta, a primitive feeling, that took no account of civilisation and good behaviour. Her heart gave an agonising throb of outraged anger and pain.

'That was a gorgeous ride, darling. Now you're home, we'll be able to go out together every morning.'

'Joss should be taking me out, not Caroline.'

In a violent upsurge of rebellion that took her completely unaware, her heart finally took control. In a few brief, devastating seconds that left her mind shaken and defeated, it put all her predetermined resolutions to flight, and came at last into its own.

'Joss is my husband, and I love him. . . .'

Although outwardly she uttered no sound, the words

echoed like a clarion call, and Netta responded as if
hypnotised. Capitulation was remarkably easy, she discovered with a numb lack of surprise. It would have been
easier still if only Joss loved her.

'My horse needs rubbing down immediately, she's
sweating.' Caroline spoke to the groom imperiously, and
tapped her riding crop against the top of her boot with a
sharp, impatient sound that sent a surge of irritation
through Netta.

'I was just about to take Fleet to the paddock, Mr Joss.
I'll only be a couple of minutes.' The groom spoke directly
to his employer, and Caroline's lips thinned in temper.

'I said immediately,' she began, and Joss broke in
quietly.

'Carry on with what you were doing, Will. I'll throw a
rug over the mare, she's still a bit blown,' he observed. 'I
warned you not to gallop her in this temperature,' he added
to Caroline, but his voice was uncritical, and he slipped the
girths with quick fingers, and pulled the saddle from the
mare's back. The animal was dark with sweat, though
Netta noticed Joss's horse was virtually unmarked.

'Don't stand right in front of the saddle rack,' he spoke
curtly to Netta, 'you can see I want to put this down.'

She could see nothing of the sort, she thought shortly,
but nevertheless she stepped out of his path to allow him
access to the rack. The saddle was heavy and awkward to
hold, but she had not even noticed the saddle rack was
there, until he mentioned it, and resentment rose like gall
in her at the sharpness of his tone.

'We'll have to get you mounted, Mrs de Courcey.' Will
freed the palomino into the paddock, and rejoined them at
the stable, and saved her from having to make any reply.
'I'll see to the mare now, sir,' he took charge of Caroline's
mount, and turned to Netta as he was about to lead it into
the stable. 'In a week or two's time, the mornings will be
nice and crisp, ideal for hacking. It's grand country for
riding hereabouts.'

'I'd love it,' Netta responded with equal enthusiasm. 'It's
ages since I've had time to ride.'

She needed time now, not so much to ride as to think. Until a few brief moments ago, her overwhelming priority had been to escape from Thimbles, and Joss. Escape from her marriage. Now, life had turned upside down again, and she felt bewildered and lost. Her fingers sought her ring, twisting it round and round on her finger. Twisting it downwards, as if she was trying to screw it on, so that it would never come off again. The jewels were all that had kept her at Thimbles until now, and the necessity to honour her promise to Ranjit to see them securely locked away in his bank in London. Now, except that she still must keep her promise, the jewels seemed unimportant—valueless. Joss had locked away her heart even more securely than the jewels, she thought bitterly, and in its turn it had erected barriers of its own which imprisoned her far more effectively than the lock on any safe could hope to do.

'You won't be able to ride,' Caroline turned on her waspishly. 'There isn't a spare horse. Fleet's in foal, and that only leaves the other two mares—Joss's and mine.'

Perhaps it was the other girl's arrogant attitude that tipped the balance, or it could have been the strange new feeling that possessed her, and seemed to dictate her actions without any conscious effort on her part. Netta did not stop to dissect her emotions, she simply acted on them without question, guided by instinct as women have been since the days of Eve. She swung round and faced Caroline, and snapped,

'Joss's mare, and *mine*,' and had the satisfaction of seeing the fair-haired girl pause, nonplussed. Now I've gone this far, I might as well carry on, she told herself stoutly, and added before Caroline could reply, 'For the short while you're a guest here,' she emphasised the other girl's position at Thimbles determinedly, 'we can hire a mount for you. I'm sure there must be a livery stables somewhere locally.' She ignored Caroline's gasp. Curiously, she felt some sympathy towards her. She knew exactly how it felt to be an unwanted outsider. Caroline looked like an alsatian that had been suddenly bitten hard by a pekinese, she thought with a detached sort of amusement, and turned to the groom.

'Will seven o'clock tomorrow morning suit you, Will?'
She tried not to notice Joss's frown, and the dawning grin
of approval which showed on the groom's face as he replied
with alacrity,

'That'll be fine, Mrs de Courcey. I'll have the mare
ready saddled up for you.'

'I'll be here by seven, then,' she nodded her thanks. 'In
the meantime,' she turned back to Joss, and her courage
very nearly failed her at the sight of the bright, glowing
flecks in his eyes. She had made him angry, but it could not
be helped. Her chin rose in a defiant tilt. She was fighting
now for her very existence, she realised bleakly. Life without Joss could hold no meaning for her, and having stirred
up her own rebellion, she thought with a grim lack of
humour, she might as well fight on, whatever the consequences—or the cost. She met his eyes without flinching. 'In the meantime, I'll start making arrangements for
the ball,' she decided in a firm voice. 'When had you in
mind to hold it?' she queried politely, knowing full well,
because she had heard Caroline discuss it with him.

'I've already made plans for next week,' the other girl
began angrily, and Netta threw her a look of glacial indifference.

Curiously, Caroline did not seem to pose so much of a
threat any longer. The real threat, Netta acknowledged unhappily, came from Joss himself. From the reason why he
had married her in the first place. From his indifference
since. She could deal with hate, she told herself forlornly.
Hate at least was a tangible emotion, something she could
have fought against. Indifference was like trying to scale a
high wall, the further up it one climbed, the higher it grew.

'In that case, the quicker I start climbing, the better,'
she told herself robustly.

'Next week is too soon for the ball,' she said aloud. 'The
week after will suit me better. I'll see Mrs Berry about it,
as soon as I go indoors. Then I'll get you to help me with
the guest list,' she added to Joss sweetly.

'Can't you and Caroline manage that between you, without dragging me into it?' Joss evinced every man's reluctance to get involved with the nitty-gritty of arrange-

ments. 'I've got months of estate work to catch up on.'

'In that case you'll be in your study,' Netta deduced, 'so I'll know where to find you.'

With a calm smile that belied the inner torment which threatened to tear her in two, she snapped her fingers to the setter and walked off towards the house with her head held high. And had to hold on tight to Tara's collar to prevent her legs from taking flight, and carrying her to the blessed privacy of some quiet corner where she could let flow the torrent of tears that, without warning, suddenly threatened to overwhelm her.

CHAPTER THIRTEEN

LONG before seven o'clock came the next morning, Netta knew she could not go riding as she planned. She also knew, with an unshakable certainty that needed no confirmation, that she would not be able to ride for several months to come.

'I've *got* to stay with Joss now. It's his child as well as mine. When I tell him....'

She paused, and her brief moment of joyous excitement vanished like morning mist.

'I won't use my baby as sticking plaster to hold our marriage together,' she told herself stubbornly. 'Joss has got to want me for myself, because he loves me—not because of our child. If he doesn't....'

If Joss became aware of her condition, she knew there would be no possibility of them parting. Clearly she remembered Wendy's words at the Embassy, minutes before the marriage ceremony.

'Joss is an honourable man....'

'But I don't want it to be that way.' Rebellion rose within her. 'I won't force myself on any man.' She gave a wry smile as she realised she had twisted Joss's own words to suit herself. She accepted her morning tray of tea and biscuits from Mary, and blessed whatever circumstance had prevented Mrs Berry from bringing it upstairs herself. The housekeeper had disconcertingly sharp eyes, whereas Mary would not question her desire to take her early morning refreshment in recumbent comfort. She would doubtless put it down to Mrs Berry's insistence that Netta must rest after her recent ordeals, and her own meek obedience in this respect would go unremarked by the young maid. For the moment at least her secret was hers alone. And must remain so for as long as possible, she determined. At least until she was sure where her future lay, either with Joss—or without. If he wanted her to remain, it must be on her own terms. Otherwise....

The bright morning outside the windows looked suddenly bleak, and she sipped gratefully at the warmth of her cup of tea to combat the icy chill that took possession of her. Her heart had started the rebellion, but it was she who would have to fight its battles, she realised ruefully. Undoubtedly, the first clash would be with Joss himself, when he discovered she had not turned up at the stables that morning. He had heard her ask Will to prepare the horse in readiness. Cravenly, she hoped he would be occupied by estate work. That he might not appear at breakfast time. That he might have eaten his meal early, and gone out. She moved slowly down the stairs, her eyes apprehensively on the breakfast room door, but it was closed, and told her nothing. She passed beneath the portrait of the first Jocelyn de Courcey, and something made her glance upwards. The painted gold stare seemed to attract her, hold her.

'You'd have battled for what you wanted, wouldn't you?' she exclaimed softly. 'You wouldn't turn and run.' A sudden sense of oneness with Joss's long-ago ancestor flooded over her, and she nodded to him companionably. 'Neither will I,' she promised, and continued on her way with renewed courage. There was no sound from the breakfast room, and no sign of Mrs Berry or Mary serving. Perhaps Joss was not there, after all? She pushed open the door and went in.

Joss was there, and one glance at his set face told her that he already knew of her defection. He must have been waiting for her, because he turned the second she walked through the door, and she knew a moment's swift thankfulness that her early morning weakness was gone. To her relief, the tea and biscuits had worked as effectively this morning as they had done the day before, and as she turned to face Joss, all traces of her early malaise had vanished. He spoke curtly, the moment she appeared.

'You said you were coming riding. Will prepared the mare ready for you.'

He was in riding kit himself. He had obviously been for a canter, and just as obviously he was very angry that she had opted out of doing the same. If she had felt well enough, she could have gone with him. Her heart wept at the loss, and she had difficulty in keeping her voice steady as she replied,

'I changed my mind.'

'You changed your mind? After you'd given Will definite instructions to get the mare ready for you by seven o'clock, you changed your mind? Just like that?' His voice flicked her like a whiplash, and she flinched away as if he had struck her a physical blow.

'I didn't. . . .' She stopped. She could not tell him she did not feel well when she woke. It would mean questions—and explanations. Joss paused for neither.

'You didn't intend to come in the first place,' he accused her angrily. 'You only ordered the horse for yourself, so that Caroline shouldn't be able to ride.'

'Nothing was further from my mind,' she denied hotly.

'Don't make excuses,' he cut her short impatiently. 'It was nothing but childish spite, on your part, to prevent Caroline from enjoying her ride. There could be no other reason for you not to turn up at the stables.'

There was an excellent reason, but it was not one she dared to divulge to Joss.

'I heard you come down, Mrs de Courcey, so I thought I'd bring in breakfast while it was nice and hot.' Mrs Berry's appearance put an end to any further conversation between them as she wheeled the trolley into the room and began loading the sideboard. 'Miss Caroline asked for her breakfast in her room as she's not riding this morning,' she explained, and anger stirred in Netta. Caroline could have her breakfast in bed, but Joss refused to let Netta have her dinner brought up on a tray the evening before.

'That's all right, if you can cope?' Joss answered the housekeeper mildly, and the latter nodded, although her expression seemed to Netta to be the reverse of enthusiastic over the extra work entailed.

'I'll manage,' she said, and turned to Netta. 'Will you

help yourself, Mrs de Courcey, or would you like me to serve for you?' she offered helpfully.

'Netta will cope for us both,' Joss answered for her, and his tone was hard.

'Then I'll leave you in peace to enjoy your meal.'

Netta could have laughed at the irony of her choice of expression. Peace was the last thing Mrs Berry had left behind her when she walked out of the room. She turned towards the sideboard, resenting what amounted to an order from Joss, but thankful for the excuse to present her back to his angry countenance.

'Porridge?'

They might have been strangers, conversing politely to one another in some hotel.

'Coffee?'

She handed Joss his bowl. He handed her a filled cup.

'Aren't you eating?'

She did not think he would notice.

'I don't want....' She stopped. She would have to eat properly, now. She had not got only her own health to consider. Besides, food would give her the strength to face the day ahead, she was under no illusion that it would be anything but difficult.

'I'll just have porridge.' It was smooth and creamy, and slipped down easily without needing much help from her aching throat. Like the early morning tea, it was warm and comforting, and by the time she had finished her helping she did indeed feel stronger, and more able to summon up the courage to bridge the tight silence which stretched between them like an invisible barrier. She asked, in what she hoped was a reasonably calm voice,

'Will you be in your study this morning?' She did not even know where his study was, she realised with a pang. 'I need to know who to invite to the ball.'

'If you still insist on taking the arrangements out of Caroline's hands,' Joss frowned impatiently. 'She could have sent out the invitations without reference to me. She knows all the people who're likely to come.'

'I shan't need to take up much of your time,' she insisted. She needed his time for the rest of their lives, she thought mournfully, but she could not tell him so.

'Oh well, if you must,' he capitulated ungraciously. 'It's your privilege.'

As his wife, it was her right, but she forbore to tell him that, also. It would only provoke another quarrel.

'We might as well get it over now, if you've finished eating.' Joss put down his coffee cup with a sharp click that made her wince for the safety of the fine china. 'I can't give you long, I've got to go out with Will on estate business.' His tone left her in no doubt that he considered the estate business more important than her own, and she bit her lip, but she rose with him,

'I'll come right away.' She would not need to ask the way to the study if she went along with Joss, she thought wistfully, and preceded him into a square panelled room on the other side of the hall. It overlooked the gardens and the river in the distance, and she viewed her surroundings interestedly. This room, more than any of the others in the house, would reveal Joss to her. It was opposite the breakfast room, and larger in size, but the panelling was similar, each separate plank being craftsman carved in the characteristic linenfold pattern of the period.

There the similarity with the other rooms ended. The elegant furnishings and sumptuous comfort that characterised the rest of the house were conspicuous by their absence. The study furnishings were strictly functional, serving the needs of a busy office on an extensive and well run estate. A solid oak desk dominated the room, its antiquity doing nothing to detract from its workmanlike appearance. A large wheelback chair, cushioned to match the curtains, stood behind the desk. It was pushed aside, Netta noticed, as if Joss had already been working there that morning after he returned from his ride, and only broke off because of the necessity of eating breakfast. The rest of the room reflected the appearance of the desk. Enclosed bookcases, filled with what looked like bound ledgers, lined the whole of one wall, and Netta's eyes were attracted to the dates, boldly embossed on the leather spines. The set of books nearest to her encompassed the 1840s, one for each year. The sheer number of the volumes on the tightly packed shelves told her that the wall held a fascinating history of careful husbandry spanning the centuries. It was something she longed to delve into. Would she ever have the opportunity? she wondered.

She gave a sharp sigh and turned her back on the books, then her eyes caught the gleam of a safe in the far corner of the room. It was square, and solid, and looked about as impregnable as Fort Knox.

'Yes, that's where your suit is.' Joss caught the direction of her glance, and his voice was as hard as the steel the safe was made of. 'And if that's the reason you were so insistent on coming into my study yourself for the address book,' the look he turned on her was one of flint, and the tiny amber specks in his eyes burned like fire, 'I might as well make it clear to you now that the safe's got a combination lock—and only I know the combination. And your safari suit, and the jewels, will remain in the safe until I personally hand them over to your father on his return to England.' Grimly he reiterated his earlier intention.

'Nothing was....' Angry crimson rose in a tide across Netta's throat and cheeks, and her eyes sparked at this further unjust assumption. The possibility had not occurred to her. She had not even thought about the jewels.

'Nothing was further from your mind,' he finished the sentence for her with harsh mockery. 'You told me that before. I didn't believe you then, and I don't believe you now. Yes, come in?' He broke off as a confident rap sounded on the study door.

'You said to come in after breakfast, Mr Joss.' Will appeared round the door and threw Netta an apologetic glance. 'I didn't mean to disturb you, Mrs de Courcey. I'll come back a bit later.'

'There's no need, Will, I've finished.' With a supreme effort Netta managed to summon up a smile. 'We're planning to hold a ball, and I just came in for the address book,' she explained as the groom still hesitated. 'I want to make out the invitations.'

'It seems a shame to stay indoors writing, on such a lovely morning,' Will said sympathetically, and turned to Joss. 'The one mare wasn't exercised earlier on, sir, so I harnessed her to the trap to give her a run. I thought as we were going down as far as the ten acre, it would be quicker than walking. Why not come along for the ride, before the sun gets too hot?' he suggested to Netta kindly. 'You looked a bit peaky yesterday morning,' he remembered, 'maybe a bit of fresh air, sitting in the trap, would help. It'll take less energy than riding.'

Will had guessed why she had not turned up at the stables, even if Joss did not. Netta saw his head come up at the groom's mention that she had been 'a bit peaky', and his look seemed to sear her across the room.

Let him make what he pleased of it, she thought defiantly. He had not waited for her to explain. She ignored the reality that she dared not offer him the true explanation. She did not feel like being just, she still smarted too much under his infamous assumption of her reason for wanting to visit his study. He had actually implied that she might try to break into his safe. Her blood boiled at the suggestion. He had accused her of being a jewel thief, once. Her lips set. She would rather waste the sunshine than ride in the trap with Joss. If Will had been going on his own she would have delighted at the opportunity for the ride. But not with Joss. She opened her mouth to refuse.

'That's an excellent suggestion.' Once again Joss spoke for her, and she bridled resentfully. She was quite capable of answering any questions addressed to her, for herself, she fumed inwardly, prevented by the presence of the groom from saying so out loud to Joss himself. 'Fresh air blows away a lot of cobwebs,' he added obliquely, and directed a look at Netta that made her grit her teeth to prevent the words on the tip of her tongue from flooding out.

'Leave the address book until we come back. You can collect it on your way indoors.' He effectively prevented her from having any excuse to refuse, since she did not know where he kept the address book in any case, and would have to wait for him to give it to her.

'The trap's outside the door, Mr Joss.'

The jet mare which Caroline had ridden the previous morning was harnessed between the shafts. Will walked to her head and held her rock-steady while Joss opened the door at the rear of the high vehicle and helped Netta to mount the step. His fingers closed over her hand with a firm grip. Assisting her? Or making sure she came with him? His hold felt warm and strong, and for an agonised second she stood still on the step and closed her eyes, fighting down a fierce longing to clasp his fingers to her, cling to them, and turn into his arms, ignore the presence of the groom and let the words fall from her lips that were so different from those that lay there just a moment ago.

'Joss! Oh Joss, I love you!'

Surely—surely he must feel her unspoken cry? But all he said was,

'Walk on, right to the front, it's quite safe.'

He misunderstood her hesitation, assumed it to be nervousness as the trap rocked slightly under her weight. She opened her eyes again and stepped in obediently and walked to the front of the trap. And the sun shone, and the birds sang, and Will's homely face smiled encouragingly at her from beside the horse's head, and with a numb sense of disbelief she saw that the world went on behaving quite normally, no matter that her heart broke in two inside her.

The trap was the bucket type, with high wheels and room for four passengers, and Joss mounted after her. He continued to hold her hand until she sat down, when he sat beside her, leaving the opposite seat for Will to take the reins, and for a wild moment of hope Netta thought he might forget to release her fingers. Perhaps not even want to loose them.

'Let's go that way, Will, down the drive and alongside the river, then come back across the park from the ten acre. It'll take us by all the growing fields, then.' Joss dropped her hand to point out the route to Will, and the sun seemed to go in. Netta shivered, and went very still.

'Are you cold?' He must have felt her shiver, the confined space forced them to sit close together, and her slight movement must have transmitted itself to him.

'No, it's....' She stammered to a halt.

'It's cool here, we're standing in the shadow of the house.' Will found her excuse for her as he joined them in the trap and unhooked the reins from the metal upright on the front. 'The sun's hot enough out of the shadow,' he consoled. 'Giddup!' He clicked his tongue to the mare and they moved smoothly across the gravel into the warm brightness away from the house, that in spite of its strength still could not melt the ice that closed about her heart with an iron grip. She winced as they passed by the clump of hollyhocks. She could not shut her eyes as she would have liked to, in case Joss noticed, so she turned her face away and pretended to admire the view, because she found the ice could not freeze away the pain.

'They keep love in the house, do hollyhocks....'

'Tara's waiting for us.' Will broke the silence and drew their attention to the setter, quietly sitting at the bend of the drive, cleverly anticipating their arrival and their route.

'Shall we stop to pick her up?' Netta begged. It would be a comfort to feel the dog with her. She needed something to hold, now Joss had loosed her hand.

'Tara won't sit in the trap with us,' Will laughed the idea out of court. 'She's much too energetic for that. She prefers to run alongside until she hears a rustle in the hedge, then she'll go off on her own, to investigate. She'll catch up with us again, along the way,' he predicted, as the trap bowled along at a smart pace, and the setter veered off after a couple of hundred yards and disappeared into the fields.

If only she had felt happier, she would have enjoyed every minute of the drive, Netta thought, looking around her. The casual clip-clop of the mare's hooves made a lazy accompaniment to the screaming swifts which wheeled and dived above them. Silver-green barley, and the pale ash blonde of oats, lay on either side as they turned across parkland, moving deeper into the estate. Ideal riding country, as Will told her. The groom slowed the horse to a walk, and smiled across at Netta.

'It's smooth enough when you're in the saddle, but it gives you a shaking up if you go too fast over the sward in the trap.'

'It's comfortable enough,' she responded. His considerate action ensured the jolting was kept to a minimum, and the high wheels cushioned any bumps so that she hardly noticed them. 'It's so peaceful, after Lak,' she responded to the groom's desire to talk. Anything was better than listening to her own thoughts. If only her heart could soak in some of the quiet that surrounded them, she thought wistfully. Instead, it seemed to have drawn to itself the turmoil of that unhappy country. 'It seemed to be all destruction and hate, out there,' her eyes darkened at the memory. 'They even burned a hillside of growing bushes, in a land where there was hardly any greenery. It seemed such a waste.' She did not tell him why the rebels fired it. It did not seem important now.

'Aye,' Will digested the information with a serious face. 'Them as makes war reaps a wild harvest,' he said sentiently, and reined the horse to a halt beside a gateway leading into a field of wheat, dark gold, and ripe for gathering.

'I reckoned we'd start to cut next week, if the weather holds,' he suggested to Joss. 'I've booked the combines, but I've got to confirm by tomorrow morning, and I thought I'd see what you said first.'

'It looks about right. Let's go and see.' Joss unlatched the door at the back of the trap and started to dismount.

'I'd better not come, because of leaving Mrs de Courcey in the trap on her own,' Will began.

'You needn't worry about me,' Netta told him confidently, 'I'll take over the reins for you, if you like.'

'If you're sure?' Will still looked doubtful, and Netta laughed his fears to rest.

'I'm positive,' she told him firmly. 'I've done quite a lot of driving in the States, with trotting horses, and they were a good deal faster than your mare's likely to be.'

'In that case....' Reassured, the groom handed her the reins and joined Joss, and left to herself, Netta relaxed. The two men walked across to the field gate, swung it open, and went inside. She saw first Joss and then Will reach out and pluck an ear of corn each and rub it between their fingers, judging its ripeness and quality. She heard Joss speak and Will answer him, discussing the coming harvest, but it was a background noise along with the rustle of the grain that bowed in shifting waves to the light wind. Her mind dismissed it, and instead turned inwards, wrestling with her own problem. Her thoughts went round and round like caged mice on an exercise wheel, seeking a solution, and finding none, and with a weary sigh she slumped back in her seat and let the reins go slack in her fingers, and the mare dropped her head to browse among the herbage of the hedge bank for green delicacies to while away the waiting.

It happened without warning.

Out of the corner of her eye Netta vaguely registered a sinuous russet body coursing the hedge, but she took little notice. Will said the setter would rejoin them, and she watched idly as Tara headed in the direction of the horse and trap, threading her way through the growth in the hedge bottom, the waving fronds of wild parsley marking her track, and her nose eagerly dropped to seek out hidden signs of life. She was almost on top of the crouching pheasant when it exploded upwards with a harsh croak of alarm, and blundered in panic flight straight into the face of the browsing mare.

The horse gave a whinny of fright and shied violently. It reared backwards, the trap tilted at a terrifying angle, and Netta grabbed at the side to save herself from sliding out through the rear doorway, which swung outwards because Will had not bothered to latch it properly when he joined Joss. With quick presence of mind she tightened her hold on the reins with her other hand and pulled in the slack as the mare's front hooves slipped wildly on the sloping bank. Gently she applied pressure on the leathers, and the mare scrabbled backwards on to terra firma again, and

Netta let out a breath of relief—but it changed to a cry of dismay as the trap rocked back on to an even keel and the rear door swung inwards again and slammed to with a sharp, resounding bang.

It was too much for the mare. Beset by unprovoked, feathered assault, and what must have sounded like a gun-shot from the rear, she tossed valour to the winds and bolted across the open parkland. Behind her, Netta heard Joss shout,

'Netta, hang on! Hang on....'

And simultaneously, Will's bawled injunction, 'Pull her in, ma'am. Pull her in!'

'I can't do both at once!' A surge of sudden anger gave her strength—anger at being shouted at. She did not stop to rationalise the reason. Fright touched the limit of her overcharged emotions, and fury boiled over inside her. With a quick movement that in her saner moments she would never have dared to attempt, she swung to her feet in the wildly swaying trap. The seemingly smooth sward of the parkland hid hitherto unsuspected hillocks, and the high wheels of the vehicle bounced across their curves like rubber balls. It was physically impossible to hold on, as Joss told her, and apply pressure on the reins at the same time, and some instinct made her choose the reins. One hand did not have the necessary power, she needed two, and all her strength. Joss or Will might have managed it, but Netta did not possess the iron-hard muscles of the men, or the necessary height, and in self-defence, to save herself from being rattled about like a single pea left in a pod, she braced herself on her feet so that her knees took the jolts like the springs of a car.

Horror descended on her as the ride of trees loomed in front of her, racing towards her at dreadful speed. And just beyond lay the wide gleam of the river. Netta knew a moment of sheer panic as they headed straight towards an enormous horse-chestnut.

'I'll never see Joss again!' She closed her eyes, and her mind went blank. For some reason she did not stop to dis-sect, she still clung to the reins. They were the only things she had, to cling to. She could not cling to Joss. She would never be able to cling to Joss again. Looking back afterwards, she wondered perhaps if it was the uneven pressure she applied on the reins in extremis, not caring how she pulled on the leathers, so long as she pulled.

She felt the trap veer to one side, and her eyes flew open again in added alarm. Was it going to tip over? She stared with a dreadful fascination as the mare started to turn away from the row of trees, that seemed to present a solid wall of living wood against them. Slowly, agonisingly slowly, the horse began to veer in a wide arc, and despair touched Netta.

'She'll never turn in time!'

The twigs from one of the lower branches of the horse-chestnut actually touched her hair, and then, seconds before the trap must surely have splintered to pieces against the trunk of the tree, the mare straightened out and raced parallel with the ride of trees, running uphill, and away from the river, instinctively heading for home and the known safety of her stable. The ground rose steeply away from the water, and it was this, and the heat of the sun, combined with the steady pull of the reins, that finally slowed the wild undisciplined gallop, first to a canter, then a trot, and then,

'Thank goodness!'

Abruptly Netta's anger deserted her, and with it her courage. She groped for the seat behind her, and dropped into it as the mare slowed to a trembling walk. She was in no better state than the horse, she realised ruefully. She shook all over.

'I'll never make a Boadicea!'

An hysterical desire to laugh and cry at the same time took possession of her, almost overwhelmed her, and it was only the sound of running feet, and Will breathlessly exclaiming in broad country parlance, fright and haste making him forget his more careful English, 'Bye, but tha' did well to pull her in like that! Tha' did real well,' that prevented her from succumbing. She took a deep, steadying breath as the groom ran to the mare's head, while Joss came over the back of the trap in an agile vault that ignored the easier, slower way through the door. He landed lightly beside her, and impulsively Netta turned towards him, her hands reaching out to him, seeking the reassurance of his hold. But instead of grasping them, and uttering the words of comfort she ached to hear, he remained apart, rebuffing her advance. She looked up into his face and checked, appalled. His eyes bored down into hers, and they glowed like coals in a face that was white under his tan.

'Surely he can't be angry with me, because of this? It wasn't my fault that the mare bolted.' Her throat closed into silence, choking back the words, and her hands dropped back on to her lap, and numb despair gripped her as he shouted,

'Why on earth did you let the mare browse like that? Will and I would only have been gone for about five minutes. Was it too much to ask, that you kept the horse standing quiet for that short time? Look at the lather she's in!' He gestured furiously towards the mare.

'How was I to know Tara would put up a pheasant right in her face?' Her anger returned, stung back into life by his tone. He had not criticised Caroline for deliberately galloping the mare the day before, and getting her into the same state, yet he blamed her—Netta—for something she could neither foresee nor prevent.

'If you'd bothered to hold her in check properly, instead of letting the reins go slack, she wouldn't have had her nose to the bank, and the bird would have flown over her.'

'And she'd have bolted, just the same,' she retorted hotly.

'She'd have been less likely to bolt if you'd kept a tight rein on her,' he thrust back angrily. 'You might have been killed!'

They might both have been killed. Herself, and her baby. A cold chill descended on Netta, and she started to tremble again. Joss would be even angrier if he knew about the baby.

'I'm surprised you even bother to think about what might have happened to me,' she flared back bitterly. 'Go and look after your mare, she seems more important to you than I am.' She turned her shoulder on him abruptly. She heard his sharp hiss of breath, but she kept her head averted. She could not continue to face him for much longer, and still remain calm. Tears rode on the back of her anger as reaction set in, and she dared not allow herself to break down in front of him. If she did, she would not be able to find the strength to hold back the longing of her heart. She would have to let it pour out its love, and then he would know....

'He'd have been concerned if it had been Caroline, instead of me.' Deliberately she whipped her anger into life again, desperately drawing round her the only armour she had left, to prevent her from blurting out her feelings, begging him to love her in return—and risking his rejection, that would turn the rest of her life into an empty waste of time. The silence seemed to stretch for ever. Her neck ached with the effort of keeping her head turned away from him. And then the trap rocked sharply as he made a swift, impatient movement.

'I'll do just that,' he ground out, and left the vehicle by the same method he used to get in. He leapt lightly over the side, she hardly heard any sound as he landed on soft-soled shoes, and he did not look at her as he passed the front of the trap on his way to the mare.

'Heel, Tara!' He checked the setter's tendency to roam with a curt command, and took the mare's head leather from Will, a move which effectively kept his back turned towards her. With soft words of encouragement to the horse, such as Netta would have sacrificed the earth to have heard addressed to herself, and which nearly succeeded in destroying her hard-won self-control because they were not, he coaxed the mare at a gentle pace towards the distant house.

'Now I know how the prisoners in the tumbrils must have felt,' she thought bleakly, riding alone and ignored in the trap behind. Accused—found wanting—and condemned, with not even the opportunity to speak in her own defence.

'It's hopeless. I might as well stop trying.'

The combined effects of misery and shock made the shadow cast across the gravel by the approaching house seem even darker than when they started out, and colder, too, symptomatic of the bleakness that touched her spirit. She shivered uncontrollably as Joss halted the trap by the front door. With a quiet word he gave the horse to Will to hold, and turned back towards the trap, and Netta galvanised into action. Dread gave her renewed strength. He must not touch her. If he did, all her resolve would vanish. She pushed herself to her feet and somehow managed to remain there, fumbling at the catch of the trap door. With shaking fingers, she forced it open and gained the gravel without help, but she was not in time to escape into the house, as she intended. Joss rounded the end of the trap, and took hold of her arm.

'You're still trembling.' The shudders that shook her were intensified by the feel of his fingers round her arm. She felt a wild urge to pull away from him, and controlled it with difficulty because of the presence of the groom. To relieve her tension, she snapped,

'It's hardly surprising if I am trembling, after what happened!' He might show some sign of concern for her, she thought angrily.

'If you must go chariot riding across the park....' he shrugged.

'It was hardly a joy-ride. And it wasn't through any fault of mine,' she blazed back.

'That's a matter of opinion,' he replied cryptically, and opened his study door. 'You said you wanted the address book.' He dismissed her ordeal, and followed her into the room, and her overwrought nerves gave way.

'You could at least say you're glad I wasn't hurt!' she cried furiously, and he straightened up from the desk and threw her a level glance. His hand closed the drawer with a dull slap, and the address book echoed it with a much louder one that made her jump as he dropped it with slow deliberation on to the desk top. She drew in a quick, apprehensive breath. His eyes were like flint, and his voice about as hard, and suddenly she longed to turn and run, only she found her legs would not obey her, because they trembled even more at the expression on his face than they had at the end of what he casually termed her chariot ride.

'I'm glad you weren't hurt,' he repeated her words after her with brittle emphasis, and went on silkily, 'but if you don't believe me—if you want proof—you can have it.'

She could not escape him this time, either. Her legs refused to carry her away, and she stood rooted to the spot as he reached her with one quick stride. She stared at him as if mesmerised, helpless to dodge away from him.

'I'm *very* glad you weren't hurt,' he mocked, and bent his head above her. Netta tried to push him away, but when her hands touched his arms they clung there instead and refused to let go. She longed to cry out, 'Stop!' but because of the relentless pressure of his lips the only sound she could utter was a low moan, and treacherously her heart did not want him to stop. With a wild beating it begged him to go on until her puny rebellion should cease, and she acknowledge that if it was anger that made him put his arms round her, it was better that than he should not hold her at all.

'Is that the proof you wanted?' He let her go at last, and she swayed against the side of the desk for support, and shook in every limb.

'Joss ... I....' She swallowed hard and tried again, her lips too numb to form the words at her first attempt.

'Go up to your room and lie down.' He spoke first, curtly. He said 'your room' not 'our room', and it was her own fault he called it that. Her pride had denied her his closeness, and now she had no pride left, and her opportunity was gone. 'I'll send Mrs Berry up to you with a hot drink.'

She longed to cry out, 'I don't want Mrs Berry, I want you.' But perversely, her dry throat and aching lips prevented her utterance, and she listened in numb silence as he went on,

'You can take the address book with you, if you still want it.' He slid it across the desk towards her. 'Unless you'd rather I gave it to Caroline to finish?' His tone said he would prefer she gave it to Caroline, and sudden hot rage flooded strength back into her limbs and gave her back the use of her voice.

'It's not Caroline's place to do the invitations. It's mine,' she spat at him furiously. 'I'll be the hostess at your celebration ball.' The words held a bitter mockery. There was nothing for her to celebrate, and she rushed on recklessly, ignoring the grim set of his jaw, 'I'll observe the conventions in front of your guests. That's what you wanted, isn't it? That's what you told me you wanted. And afterwards....'

Tears choked her voice, and she bent swiftly and snatched the address book from off the desk, holding it in front of her like a shield, to ward off what she scarcely knew.

'And afterwards ... what?' Joss enquired icily, and his eyes were twin fires that she could not meet, because she dared not contemplate life afterwards. Life without Joss.

She gave a strangled sob and spun away from him, pulling at the handle of the study door with frantic fingers. It swung open and she ran through, and without waiting for it to shut she fled for the stairs. She was half way up them when the door banged to behind her, and the echo of it resounded through the quiet hall, slamming shut on her most precious dreams.

CHAPTER FOURTEEN

SHE did not go down to the stables again. She knew Joss went riding, because she heard him moving about in his dressing room very early each morning. On occasions, the hands of her bedside alarm stood at exactly six o'clock when his door closed behind him, but he did not ask her to go with him, which was a relief and a pain at the same time. Caroline accompanied him once, Netta watched them from her window as they cantered side by side across the park, but when Joss persisted in his early start it proved too much for his cousin, who desisted with a very bad grace.

'Can't you do your work first, and then come riding at a more reasonable time?' she pouted illhumouredly at breakfast one morning. 'Surely you needn't go out at such an unearthly hour?'

'Once I start on estate work in the morning, I don't want to have to break off for anything except meals,' Joss answered her firmly. 'It's either an early ride, or none at all, at least for the moment until I've caught up with the backlog of paper work that's piled up since I've had to spend so much time abroad,' he grimaced. He evidently took the management of his estate seriously, and Netta could sympathise with his need to clear away the outstanding debris, even if Caroline could not. It was not an enviable chore, and the longer it was delayed the worse it would become as other tasks superimposed their own demands on his attention. He treated her own modest request for his time with unconcealed impatience.

'I've done the invitations, ready for posting.' She handed him a neatly scripted list. 'I'd like you to look down the names, in case there are any you disagree with.' She did not know his friends or his relations. One or two of the names in the address book she recognised as her father's clients, but the rest were just names, and the lack

of recognition hurt her intolerably. 'I've clipped some
blank cards to the list, in case you want to add any.' She
had left a dozen blank cards, and he picked up her list
with a gesture of irritation.

'Is it absolutely necessary to bother me with these?' he
frowned. 'Surely you and Caroline between you could
attend to the arrangements?'

'I could have done it easily, if I'd been asked,' Caroline
put in sweetly, and Joss's frown grew deeper as her meaning penetrated.

'In that case, *I'll* ask you, *now*.' He tossed Netta's carefully written list across the breakfast table to his cousin,
and drained the last of his cup of coffee preparatory to returning to his study. 'I haven't the time to attend to it myself this morning.'

Netta drew in a quivering breath, then slowly she began
to count. One ... two ... three....

'I won't retaliate,' she vowed. 'I won't. ...' She could not
afford too many emotional upsets now, the precious life she
bore was worthy of better treatment, and was infinitely
more valuable to her than any temporary satisfaction she
might derive from giving Caroline or Joss a verbal thrash-
ing, and she battled to subdue her natural inclinations. She
longed to scream—to hit out at Joss and Caroline—to
throw things. To break her second cup of coffee, still pip-
ing hot, over Joss's insensitive head. With an effort that
was to cost her a raging headache half an hour later, she
did none of these things. 'I mustn't give way. Some time,
I've got to learn not to let it matter.' It would be easier
when she was no longer at Thimbles, no longer in reach of
the sound of Joss's voice, of the accidental touch of his
hand against her own as they passed the salt, the marma-
lade....

'I'll use the spare invitation cards myself, to bring in
one or two of my own friends,' Caroline decided, and
Netta gritted her teeth. Caroline should have asked, not
stated. Joss did not seem to notice the omission, he merely
nodded indulgently.

'Yes, do that. You'll find envelopes and stamps in my

study.' He had not offered these facilities to Netta, and Caroline did not afterwards seem to think it was necessary to mention who it was she had invited, or even how many.

'I won't give her the satisfaction of asking,' Netta told herself determinedly, and racked her brains to circumvent the inconvenience of not knowing. Her lack of precise knowledge of numbers was the biggest hurdle.

'A buffet supper, that's the answer,' she hit on the ideal solution triumphantly. 'Numbers won't matter then.'

In fact, among the sixty or so guests who turned the long ballroom at Thimbles into a kaleidoscope of vividly coloured evening gowns, complemented by the magpie black and white of the men's evening dress, the half dozen or so of Caroline's friends who turned up did not make much difference, although they were instantly recognisable, Netta noticed. The women's hair and dress and make-up were just a shade too bright, and the men too obviously prosperous, and their laughter a note too loud, to mix easily with the other guests, and they remained as they came, in a clique apart.

Joss's face was impassive as he stood with Netta at the entrance to the ballroom to greet them. She had contemplated buying a dress of her own for the occasion, but it meant asking Joss for money, and for transport to go into the nearest town, and rather than do either she once again resorted to raiding Rosemary's emergency wardrobe, and blessed her absent sister-in-law for providing her with just the right dress for the occasion.

It was in pure silk, of a delicate silvery green, with a high neckline and tiny cape sleeves. The cool shade showed off her tan to perfection, and the soft, flowing lines of the skirt whispered as she walked. The style did not call for much jewellery, and she reversed her watch so that the gold band made a bracelet. That, and her wedding ring, would be sufficient, she decided. She would not ask Joss for adornments, either.

She felt him glance down at her as she joined him at the entrance to the ballroom. She did not join him until the last minute. The less time they spent together, the less likely they were to quarrel, she acknowledged drearily, and she wanted tonight to go as smoothly as possible. She had spared herself no effort to make the evening perfect. The ball was the only thing she had been able to do for Joss—except marry him, she thought wryly—and if the latter had turned out to be a disaster, at least she intended to see that the former was a success. Caroline criticised the arrangements, but she had not expected anything less.

'Do we *have* to have a string orchestra?' she complained. 'Can't we have something a bit livelier?' The intrumentalists Netta chose were a small, exclusive band known to her through various functions she herself had attended in London, and their music set the seal on any gathering.

'It's the one I've chosen.' She refused to budge from her initial decision.

'It isn't only the music, it's the supper as well,' Caroline appealed to Joss. 'I'd have thought a proper dinner would have been more in keeping with the occasion.'

'Since you didn't think fit to tell me how many guests you'd invited, a buffet meal was the only possible choice,' Netta silenced her effectively, and looking round the assembled gathering, from her position at Joss's side, she was glad she had stood firm. The musicians, the flowers, the whole elegant gathering, with the possible exception of Caroline's guests, fitted at Thimbles. Her choice had been instinctively right, and on that, at least, she could feel satisfied. She joined Joss only seconds before the first guests arrived, and her heart sank as she noticed the specks in his eyes glow as he looked at her.

'You're. . . .' he began, and his voice sounded tight.

'I'm not late,' she denied angrily, before he could go any further. 'You said eight o'clock, and it's exactly that now.' She reversed her wrist so that he could see her watch face, and at the same time gave away her strategy as regarded jewellery, or its lack.

'You haven't a proper bracelet.' He noticed immediately.

'I've got all I need.' Proudly she scorned to borrow more, and turned away from the fire in his eyes to force a smile she did not feel for the benefit of the first arrivals. For the next half hour there was no time for any private conversation as their guests flowed through the door in a constant stream. Her right hand was shaken until it ached. She knew just how celebrities must feel, she thought ruefully, flexing her tingling fingers behind her back as yet another party of people she had invited, and yet did not recognise, came through the big double doors to greet them.

In swift succession she found herself kissed, congratulated and questioned in the friendliest manner, and when there were no more guests left to arrive she realised, with a heart that broke at the sheer irony of it all, that Joss's relations and closest friends accepted her, even if Joss did not.

'Shall we open the ball?'

He swept her into his arms. He looked incredibly handsome in evening dress. The stark black and white enhanced his already distinguished appearance and those looking on must have thought she was the luckiest woman in the world. How wrong they were! she thought bitterly. But her heart did not listen to her denial, it quickened in a way that had nothing to do with the beat of the music as Joss guided her expertly along the gleaming expanse of floor that opened up in front of them as their guests followed the time-honoured tradition, and parted on either side to allow them the opening dance.

'You dance well,' he said.

'So do you,' she responded politely.

Banalities, even if they were true. Stiffly formal, keeping them apart. But she discovered that even unhappiness could not hold the music at bay. Netta was a natural dancer, and Joss's performance was a polished equal of her own, and the music drew them both like Pan pipes, beckoning, insistent. He held her firmly, but not too tightly, and her heart cried out to him to tighten his hold, crush her if he wanted to, as loving him had crushed her heart until it was like a withered sponge, fit only to be thrown away. Without conscious thought she adjusted herself to his hold, and allowed the tempo of the music to carry her along, drugging her into an oblivion that obliterated her surroundings, her guests, everything but the fact that she was in Joss's arms.

They reached the end of the room and he turned her once, twice, making the skirt of her dress billow in a soft, whispering cloud of silver-green about her feet. The notes of a violin rose high and sweet, throbbing a message she did not want to hear—dared not listen to. . . .

'Some enchanted evening, you may see a stranger. . . .' She had seen a stranger, and——

'Joss, oh, Joss, I love you!'

She rested her cheek against his lapel, and closed her eyes, but she could not shut out the tune. It haunted her, like the sound of the official's voice in the Embassy drawing room haunted her still.

'To love and to cherish. . . .'

Like the sound of Joss's firm rejoinder,

'I do.'

It was so real, she could even smell the heady, overpowering perfume of the tua lilies. It flowed about her in cloying sweetness, and her feet missed the rhythm, and she stumbled and would have fallen but for Joss's arms, which instantly tightened round her.

'Has your sandal come undone?'

'No.' Her eyes were open now, and wide with memory, and pain. 'I thought . . . just for a moment . . . I thought I smelled lilies.' It was ridiculous, of course. She had not ordered lilies in the floral decorations for the ballroom. Her voice trembled into silence.

'They're a bit overpowering, close to.' To her astonishment he did not contradict her. 'I had them put in the corner, because of their height.' He twirled her round again, so that she could see for herself the tub of lilies, their great golden heads spotted with brown velvet blobs near the centres. Netta caught her breath.

'How could you?' He must have thought the floral decorations she ordered were inadequate, but did he *have* to supplement them with lilies, of all flowers?

The music swelled to a crescendo, and Joss did not hear. He twirled her round again to face the return journey the length of the room, and the tub of lilies was lost to her sight.

'I had them brought in from the gardens this evening. They're a bit like the tua lilies, don't you think? Or don't you remember what they looked like?'

It seemed to her an odd question to ask. How could she ever forget? Their perfume had followed her across two oceans, all the way from Lak. It tormented her dreams by night, so that she woke crying out as if from fever, and tantalised her by day like a silent wraith to which she would be chained for the rest of her life. The perfume of them followed her now, even across the length of the great ballroom, choking her, denying her air. Through a mist she saw Joss turn with a smile to acknowledge the friendly applause that followed their performance, saw the dancers close the gap as the orchestra broke into a quickstep. She swayed, and from a long way off heard someone say, in a voice she ought to recognise,

'Give Netta a drink, she's feeling dizzy.'

And Caroline's voice reply, spitefully,

'Maybe that's why she's feeling dizzy.'

'Sit down for a moment or two, and drink this.' Joss pressed her into a chair, and someone put a glass into her hand. She sipped obediently, too bemused to do anything else. She had never particularly liked wine. She did not realise until now just how much she *dis*liked it. The sharp, dry sherry stung her throat and made her cough, but it gave her an excuse for the tears that sprang to her eyes, and it revived her enough to allow her to turn and thank the woman who had given it to her, and who still stood beside her.

'Wendy!' She looked up into her friend's laughing face. 'And Harry!' She jumped to her feet, her daze vanishing. 'When did you get here?' She had not sent them an invitation, did not know they were due to arrive. 'I didn't know you were even back in this country yet.'

'We had to report to Paris first,' Harry gave her a laughing hug—a different Harry, rested and cheerful, with the troubles of Lak left far behind him.

'Joss traced us,' Wendy gurgled at the amazement on Netta's face. 'He rang us in Paris and told us about the ball, and begged us to come over. We didn't need much coaxing,' she chuckled. 'But we couldn't write and let you know, because Joss said he wanted it to be a surprise for you.'

'It's wonderful!' Netta supposed she ought to thank Joss. It was considerate of him to give her a pleasant surprise, for once, she thought cynically. And then she remembered that the Frasers were his friends as well as her own. Had he invited them in order to discuss their marriage? she wondered dully. Perhaps to ask Harry's advice on how best to get it annulled? The Frasers had been witnesses, and knew the circumstances, and the ex-Ambassador might be prepared to pull strings to obtain an annulment quickly and quietly. Perhaps Caroline had been pressing Joss.... Through the coldness that gripped her she could feel Joss standing close behind her, feel the electric currents of question and answer pass unspoken between them.

'Ranjit sent a message for you,' Harry broke across the tight silence, and Netta turned to him with quick relief.

'Is he safe? When did you hear from him?'

'Only an hour before we left Paris to come here,' her informant told her with a smile. 'And he's quite safe, and unharmed. He asked me to tell you that he intended to come to England in about three months' time, when he's had an opportunity to sort his business into some kind of order again. Oh, and he said something about having recovered most of the settings from your hotel. He said you'd understand?'

'I understand.' So did Joss. She could feel him tense, his thoughts reach out to her, meeting her own in a mental telepathy that had no need of words. Now he must know her story of how she came by the jewels was true. It had mattered to her that he knew, once. Now, she felt vindicated, and uncaring. Empty, except for an ache that grew with every hour, but it was for Joss, and not for the jewels.

'Was his business damaged much?' She found she did

not care about that either, any more, but politeness demanded that she should ask.

'Some,' Harry answered her laconically, 'but nothing that can't be mended, given time. The Government has regained control in Lak, and there's a measure of order been restored, but I'm afraid it'll be a long time before things get back to normal again. The insurgents had a field day when they ran riot, and there was a great deal of damage done, not least to the economy of the country. It seems such a pity, when they'd made such strides during the last few years in extending education and up-to-date medical treatment even into their remote mountain regions. And now the culmination of years of effort has been virtually destroyed overnight by a handful of hotheads.' The expression on his face was compounded of anger and regret. 'It'll take a decade to recoup the damage they've done.'

'Them as makes war, reaps a wild harvest. . . .'

It was as if Will's words had just been spoken aloud between them. Joss's look pierced her, silent, compelling, so that she was forced at last to turn and meet his eyes. She raised her face to his, and was lost. In one fleeting second, plucked from an ocean of time, a frail link of understanding reached out between them. She hesitated, half raised her hand in a tentative, pleading gesture. For a brief, heart-stopping minute she thought Joss might respond, might reach across and take it.

'My dance, I think.'

Harry grasped her hand. The ex-Ambassador to Lak swung her on to the floor in a well executed foxtrot, and in that moment Netta felt her life had ended. She twisted her head to look back at Joss, her heart mirrored in her eyes, but he was following Harry's example and drawing Wendy on to the dance floor, his head bent, listening as his partner chatted, and he did not see Netta look back. And then other couples danced between them, and Joss was lost to her sight. And there was only desolation, and the sickly sweet perfume of the lilies as they neared the end of the ballroom. And her own heart's wild harvest, of long-ing, and bitter regret.

'You dance like a dream,' Harry grinned when the music stopped. 'Be sure to save me another twirl later,' he de-manded.

'I will,' Netta promised, 'but just now I need a cool drink and a sit down. It's hot in here. Why don't ladies carry fans any more?' she complained.

'Come and sit over by the french windows, and I'll bring you a lemonade,' Harry offered, and led her towards where the big double windows lay open to the wide flagged ter-race leading on to the gardens.

'That's better!' She subsided thankfully on to the chair he found for her, and leaned back, breathing in the warm scented air from the garden outside. It was a fresh, essentially English sweetness, redolent of moist earth and new-mown lawns, and the free second blooming of well tended roses, refreshing to her nostrils after the heavy, cloying scent of the lilies. Harry left her in search of the lemonade, and her mind wandered. Someone had already sought the sanctuary of the terrace, she became aware of movement outside in the dusk, and half rose from her chair. She had no desire to eavesdrop, however unwittingly, on a courting couple, then she sat back again. 'There's more than one couple outside,' she realised, as her eyes be-came more accustomed to the dusk, and she picked out a group of people, four or five figures on the outer edge of the terrace. The glow of a cigarette, and the snowy gleam of a man's shirt front sprang into being against the wide stone pillars. Another man spoke, and a woman's voice answered him: Caroline's voice. The man said,

'It's a pity about the Hunt Ball. Thimbles would be an ideal place to hold it. Ideal hunting country, too, it should be well stocked with foxes if the packs have never been run across it.'

'Oh, Joss's family have got this bee in their bonnets about hunting,' Caroline replied scornfully, and Netta rose swiftly to her feet. She had no desire to listen in to other people's conversations, either. She took a couple of steps away from the windows, and Joss said,

'Sit down again.' He appeared at her side and handed her the glass of lemonade he bore in his hand. 'Our guests are enjoying the buffet, so we might as well relax for a while.' He said 'our guests' and 'we might as well relax'. Her fingers trembled as she took the glass, hazarding the liquid inside, and she sat down abruptly lest it should spill.

'I thought ... Harry said....' She foundered to a stop and stared mutely up at Joss.

'I met Harry coming back with your lemonade, so I took the glass from him and brought it instead,' he explained. 'Sit back and enjoy it,' he insisted, a superfluous injunction as it turned out, since the chair suddenly became necessary to aid the alarming weakness in her legs, that refused to allow her to stand up unsupported. She lowered her eyes to the glass, and sipped at its contents that might have been plain water for all she knew, but she was thankful to slake a throat that had suddenly gone as dry as sand. She could not look at Joss any longer, at the deep burning fire in his gold eyes that had the power to scorch her until she could have cried aloud with the pain. Surely he could not still be angry with her because she had not asked him for jewellery to wear with her dress? she thought wretchedly. And she had not been late in joining him to greet their guests, she had told him she was not late. Did he not believe her about that, either? Perhaps his wrist watch was fast, or hers might be slow.... The thoughts raced round and round in jumbled confusion through her mind, and in desperation she at last raised her head. 'I can't keep my nose buried in a lemonade glass for the rest of the evening,' she thought half hysterically, and risked an upward glance at him. He did not *look* angry, his expression was mild as he stood over her, watching her, and yet his eyes still smouldered with that inward light she had come to know so well.

'Leave the rest of your drink if you don't want it,' he suggested as she toyed nervously with the glass, unable to bring herself to drink again. 'Come and walk in the garden with me, it'll cool you off better than lemonade.'

'I'll put the glass down first.' An unaccountable, heady

excitement took possession of her, far more potent than any wine.

'Put it on the windowsill.'

'It's still half full, it might get spilled. There's a waiter coming towards us, I'll give it to him.'

She grasped for time to compose herself, to make her legs obey her will and walk beside him in the garden. She turned to put her glass on the waiter's tray, shook her head at the offer of another drink, and then turned back again in time to hear Caroline say,

'When Joss and I are married, I'll make him change his mind about letting the local hunt come across Thimbles land.'

The excitement died within her, and she felt sick. Was that why Joss wanted her to walk with him in the privacy of the garden? To tell her he intended to marry Caroline? To tell her in the dusk, because he could not face her in the light with such news? She spun round to speak to him, to tell him she would not come with him, but he had already stepped through the french windows ahead of her while she was attending to her glass, his silent tread making no sound on the smooth flags of the terrace.

'I thought Joss was married to that redhaired girl who stood with him when we came in? Who was she?' one of the men with Caroline asked, curiously.

'Oh, they're married—at the moment,' Caroline replied significantly. 'She's some little ingénue he picked up in Lak. They were caught up together in the civil uprising there. Men do quixotic things at such times. Fortunately these days they're not irreparable.'

Netta drew a hard, painful breath. It was uncanny. Caroline was explaining her marriage to Joss almost word for word as she, Netta, had predicted she would. She felt as if she was taking part in the scene of some weird play, the lines of which she had already learned by heart.

'Are you using this chair, Mrs de Courcey?' A black and white figure appeared beside her, coveting her recent seat for his partner, and she shook her head numbly. The chair found another occupant, and a burst of chatter and laughter broke out round her as men plied their partners with spoils from the buffet table, and sought a quiet corner in which to enjoy them. Tears pricked the back of her eyes, and she turned on to the dusk of the terrace to hide them.

'I might as well get it over, and have done with it,' she told herself wretchedly. And have done with Joss, too. . . . With a valiant effort she held her head high and walked out to join him, then paused irresolutely. He was strolling towards Caroline and her guests, was nearly upon them, and it was obvious the group had not heard him coming. His peculiar lightness of tread denied them any warning of his presence.

'We'll hold the Hunt Ball at Thimbles next year, never fear,' Caroline continued her conversation confidently.

'You're neglecting your guests, Caroline,' Joss spoke from just behind her, and there was ice in his voice. She spun round with a gasp, and a look of startled dismay spread across her face.

'I . . . I . . .'

'I can recommend the buffet,' he cut smoothly across what she was about to say, and instantly turned back to Netta. 'Mind the steps,' he cautioned, 'the rest is level walking, once we're on the lawns.'

He gave the group on the terrace a cool nod, and guided Netta down the shallow stone flight. She needed guidance, for the tears would no longer be denied, and they treacherously aided the deeper darkness of the garden, so that she trod blindly where he led, conscious only that the lights of the house grew dim behind them, and the noise of the ballroom faint as the garden received them into its blessed quiet, that for Netta held no peace. She shivered.

'You haven't got a wrap,' Joss realised. 'Take my jacket instead.' Without waiting for her to answer, he slipped his jacket off his own shoulders and draped it round her, then spoke softly down at her through the darkness.

'You're such a tiny thing, it's nearly an overcoat on you.'

It was warm, from the warmth of his own body, but

clothing could not combat the chill that gripped her, which came from inside her, and not from the gentle air of the end-of-summer night.

'It won't stay on.' She put up her hands to grasp at the jacket as it slipped on her too slender shoulders, in danger of falling to the ground, but Joss caught it and held it round her, pressing his hands across her shoulders and back. Holding the jacket against her. Holding her against him. She spoke hurriedly, grasping at the first subject that entered her mind, because she could not bear his closeness, knowing they were a million miles apart.

'It was kind of you to ask Wendy and Harry to come.'

'It's a relief to know they're safe. And your client, too,' he remembered their message from Ranjit.

'At least you know now, I'm not a jewel thief.' She could not disguise the bitterness in her voice, and she felt him go still.

'You *were* a thief. You are still,' he said deliberately, and she stiffened as if he had struck her. Fury seethed in her. She longed to throw off his jacket, risk the chill of the evening air, throw his words back in his face, and refute his infamous suggestion. And then he spoke again, very softly, drawing her close against him with a strength that even her anger was powerless to resist.

'You stole my heart,' he told her, so low that she had to strain to hear him. And even then her ears did not believe what they heard, so he repeated it slowly, to convince them. 'You stole my heart, the first moment I saw you, in Lak. You still possess it, and you always will, because I don't want it back.' He had given it to her to keep, freely, unreservedly.

Was she dreaming? Could it be her overwrought imagination, that made her hear words that her wildly palpitating heart had longed to hear, and so far had waited for in vain? But the music of the string orchestra played softly in the background, the lights of the house glowed distantly across the lawns, and from far away she could hear the call of a hunting owl, real, tangible things, none of them the stuff of dreams.

'Netta—darling—I love you.' His voice vibrated with urgent passion, and he strained her to him as if he feared to let her go. 'I love you—I love you. Say you love me, too?' he demanded, and now, incredibly, she knew she was not dreaming. Knew the words were real, that she had never thought to hear from his lips. 'I love you, I love you....' He thought her silence meant she did not hear him, but it only meant she wanted to hear him say it again, with ears that would never tire of hearing it repeated, never so long as she lived.

'I shouldn't have forced you into marriage,' he groaned, when she still did not speak. 'It was wrong, but I was afraid of losing you. I brought the lilies into the ballroom tonight, in the hope they might remind you—speak for me....'

'You told me you married me to get me on the plane, with the rest of the Embassy staff.' She raised her face to his, a pale flower in the darkness of the garden.

'I lied,' he confessed. 'You could have come on the plane without marrying me. But if I'd let you do that, once we reached England you might have disappeared, out of reach, and I'd have lost you. I thought if I bound you to me, at least I should be able to hope ... I wouldn't want to live, if I lost you,' he declared, and his face worked suddenly, unmanned by the thought of losing her, and with a muffled sound he lowered his head and buried his face in her curls.

'Don't!' She could not bear to see him suffer. She had suffered herself in the same way, and knew how it felt. 'I love you,' she crooned, 'I'll always love you. We'll never lose each other,' she comforted him from her newfound position of strength and confidence. 'Marriage is for ever, and so is our love.' She reached up tender hands, and drew his face down to her own, responding with a tremulous joy to the passionate pressure of his lips as they lingered on her hair, her eyes, and the soft, throbbing hollow of her throat, leaving rapture in their train, and a deep, contented joy such as she thought she would never know. With a tiny sigh she surrendered to his arms, and the quiet of the garden folded round them. Neither noticed the setter trot towards them and stop, front paw upraised, to give them a long, wise look, then turn away again, leaving them alone.

'The moment I saw you with Wendy and Harry at the Embassy, I was lost,' Joss confessed at last with a smile, and Netta raised eyes that shone, but not with tears, and knew happily that the fire that glowed deep in his gold orbs burned not only with anger, but when his heart was deeply stirred.

'I didn't give you a proper wedding ring,' he recalled remorsefully. 'And you a goldsmith's daughter, too!'

'I don't want any other ring but yours.' She nestled in the safe, warm circle of his arms like a bird that has come to rest.

'After tomorrow we'll be on our own at last,' he said contentedly. 'All our guests will have gone home, and we can be alone.' A thrill of pure happiness ran through her, at the way he said 'alone'.

'Won't Caroline . . .?'

'Caroline will leave first thing in the morning,' his tone hardened. 'I've tolerated her outrageous behaviour before, for the sake of her parents, but this time she's gone too far. She won't return to Thimbles.'

'I didn't opt out of riding that morning, just to spite Caroline. I didn't feel well when I woke. . . .' Suddenly it was important that he should believe her.

'I didn't think you did.' He kissed her tiny worry away.

'You were angry.'

'Only because I was disappointed. I'd set such store, by having that ride with you, having the chance to talk with you alone. Do you realise, since we've been married, we've hardly ever been alone?' he asked her incredulously. 'There's always been something to come between us. The jewels. . . .'

'My father can have those, he'll look after Ranjit now. You can give them to him when he comes home.' The jewels no longer mattered.

'The civil uprising. . . .'

'That's behind us now.' She had almost forgotten it, except that it gave her to Joss.

'There's always been something,' he insisted.

'Except in the cave,' she reminded him in a small, breathless voice. Would he remember, too? Desperately, she wanted him to remember.

'Ah, the cave.' His voice, his look, showed that he remembered, and they turned those few brief hours into a thing of unutterable beauty. He lowered his head and his lips reverently sealed the memory deep in her heart, so that it was a while before he recalled,

'We can ride together now, whenever you like,' he said happily. 'But if you're uneasy about riding the jet mare after she bolted on you, I'll find you another mount. You needn't feel obliged to ride her, after that. Dear heart!' he hugged her even closer to him, and his voice shook as he remembered, 'I thought for sure I'd lost you then. I was so afraid.'

'I shan't be able to ride, for a while,' she told him.

'You can have the palomino, for your own,' he laid his most precious possession at her feet, misunderstanding her hesitation, putting it down to nervousness after her ordeal in the trap. 'Fleet's as gentle as a lamb,' he reassured her, 'but she won't be ready to carry you yet.'

'When she's ready will be time enough for me.' She could give him her own news now, safe in the warm security of his love. 'Fleet's foal will be ready for riding at about the same time that our son will need his first mount.' Shyly she nestled her head against his heart, her face down-turned, even though the dusk laid gentle fingers on the soft rosy tide that warmed her cheeks and throat.

'Our ... son?'

Joss's voice died into silence, and a quick fear stabbed through Netta like a knife. Did he mind? Did he not want their child? Perhaps.... She raised her head, and the incredulous joy on his face told her that her fears were unfounded. That, and the deep, enduring tenderness that shone out from his eyes, spoke from the strength of his arms as he clasped her close to his heart in a strong, safe embrace, holding her, and their child, and their future. . . .

'You didn't let me tell you how lovely you look,' he murmured after a long, sweet time had passed between them. 'I tried to tell you, when you joined me in the ballroom tonight, but you thought I was going to say you were late coming down.'

He laughed softly at the memory, and she joined in gaily. She had been wonderfully, blissfully, on time. She started to tell him so, but his lips claimed her own, masterfully silencing the words that no longer needed to be spoken.

Masquerade
Historical Romances

Intrigue
excitement
romance

CROMWELL'S CAPTAIN
by Anne Madden

Why should Cathie Gifford, who came of a staunchly
Royalist family, feel compelled to tend the wounded
Roundhead captain? And why should a man like
Piers Denham, who had betrayed his own kind by
fighting for Parliament, be able to shake her loyalty
to the King?

HOUSE OF SATAN
by Gina Veronese

Count Anton von Arnheim's Viennese mansion was
notorious, even in the pleasure-loving society of 1785.
And into it came Eloise, the Count's innocent and
beautiful ward. How long could she go on living
happily in the House of Satan?

Look out for these titles in your local paperback shop from
12th September 1980

Doctor Nurse Romances

and September's
stories of romantic relationships behind the scenes
of modern medical life are:

FIRST YEAR LOVE
by Clare Lavenham

When Kate started her nursing career at Northleigh
Hospital, she was thrilled to recognise the consultant
surgeon as a long-time friend of her brother's. Might her
childish hero-worship now blossom into something more
mature? Or was she looking in the wrong direction
altogether?

SURGEON IN CHARGE
(Winter of Change)
by Betty Neels

Mary Jane was over twenty-one, and a competent staff
nurse, so when she inherited a fortune she was furious
to find that she also had a guardian — the high-handed
Fabian van der Blocq. But what could she do about it
— or him?

The Mills & Boon Rose is the Rose of Romance

Every month there are ten new titles to choose from — ten new stories about people falling in love, people you want to read about, people in exciting, far-away places. Choose Mills & Boon. It's your way of relaxing:

September's titles are:

WHERE THE WOLF LEADS *by Jane Arbor*
Everybody seemed to behave like sheep where Dracon Leloupblanc was concerned. And why, thought Tara Dryden indignantly, should she add herself to their number?

THE DARK OASIS *by Margaret Pargeter*
When Mrs Martin's son ran off with Kurt d'Estier's fiancée, she persuaded her secretary Maxine to go off to Morocco to try to pacify Kurt.

BAREFOOT BRIDE *by Dorothy Cork*
To save face when she found her fiancé strangely unwelcoming, Amy pretended that she was going to marry the cynical Mike Saunders instead — then Mike stunned her by taking her up on it . . .

A TOUCH OF THE DEVIL *by Anne Weale*
There was mutual attraction between Joe Crawford and Bianca — but marriage, Joe made it clear, was not in his mind.

THE SILVER THAW *by Betty Neels*
A holiday in Norway was supposed to give Amelia and her fiancé Tom a chance to get their affairs settled once and for all. But somehow she found herself seeing far more of Gideon van der Tolck.

DANGEROUS TIDE *by Elizabeth Graham*
Her ex-husband was the last person Toni had expected to meet on board a cruise ship to Mexico. But he, it appeared, had expected to meet her . . .

MARRIAGE IN HASTE *by Sue Peters*
Trapped in a Far Eastern country on the brink of civil war, Netta could only manage to escape if she married the mysterious Joss de Courcy . . .

THE TENDER LEAVES *by Essie Summers*
Searching for her father in New Zealand, Maria could have done without the help of the disapproving Struan Mandeville. But could she *really* do without Struan?

LOVE AND NO MARRIAGE *by Roberta Leigh*
Career woman Samantha swiftly fell in love with Bart Jackson, who had no time for career girls and thought she was a quiet little homebody . . .

THE ICE MAIDEN *by Sally Wentworth*
Just for an experiment, Gemma and her friends had computerised the highly eligible Paul Verignac, and Gemma was proceeding to turn herself into 'his kind of woman' . . .

If you have difficulty in obtaining any of these books from your local paperback retailer, write to:

Mills & Boon Reader Service
P.O. Box 236, Thornton Road, Croydon, Surrey, CR9 3RU.